Honeymoon

A list of the books in the series appears at the end of this volume.

HONEYMOON

Stories by
Merrill Joan Gerber

UNIVERSITY OF ILLINOIS PRESS

Urbana and Chicago

Publication of this work was supported in part
by grants from the National Endowment for the Arts
and the Illinois Arts Council, a state agency.

©1985 by Merrill Joan Gerber
Manufactured in the United States of America
C   5   4   3   2   1

This book is printed on acid-free paper.

"Honeymoon," *Sewanee Review,* vol. 42, no. 1, Winter, 1984.
"At the Fence," *Sewanee Review,* vol. 43, no. 1, Winter, 1985.
"The Mistress of Goldman's Antiques," *Virginia Quarterly Review,* vol. 55,
    no. 3, Summer, 1979.
"I Don't Believe This," *Atlantic Monthly,* vol. 254, no. 4, October, 1984.
"Witnesses," (under the title "What's A Family For?"), *Redbook,* vol. 164,
    no. 1, November, 1984.

Library of Congress Cataloging in Publication Data

Gerber, Merrill Joan.
    Honeymoon.

    (Illinois short fiction)
    I. Title.
PS3557.E664H6   1985   813'.54   84-28023
ISBN 0-252-01205-4 (alk. paper)

For Eva and Milton Hindus

Contents

Honeymoon

On their way out of the Bun Boy coffee shop in Baker, Rand gave Cheryl a quarter to buy a Bio-Rhythm fortune card from a vending machine. She stood in the hot desert wind, her skirt lashing about her legs like a whip, strands of hair flying into her mouth, while she laughingly read him the news that the bio-graph rated her low on luck, low on sex, and low on leisure plans, while it rated her high on health, endurance, and driving.

"So can I drive the rest of the way to Vegas now?" she asked. "It's so boring just to look out the window. There's no scenery."

"Get in the car, please," Rand said, his pants legs flapping like banners in a used-car lot, ". . . and don't put another ding in my door."

"I didn't put the first ding in," she said, getting into his red Corvette. She automatically took a sip of water from the insulated cup hanging in a holder on the dash and made a face. "Yuck — hot."

"You just had a milkshake," Rand said. "Why do you have to drink old water?"

"I don't know," she said, shrugging. "I just saw it there. Don't worry about it."

He pulled onto the road, and up ahead of them Cheryl saw white pom-poms on a car. "I wish we could have a 'Just Married' sign," she said. "Then everyone would look in our car when they passed us."

Rand accelerated, and Cheryl peered into the car with the pom-poms. The girl, a blonde like her, turned her head the other way when she saw Cheryl staring. The boy, who looked about the age of

Rand's son, gave her a zany grin, friendly and lewd at the same time. Cheryl waved, giggling out loud. She turned to Rand, seeing his handsome profile against the twisted joshua trees in the distance. "How could I be low on sex and leisure plans if this is my honeymoon?" she asked. She reached over and stroked his thigh. "Anyway, I've *never* been low on sex."

"How do you rate on money?" Rand asked.

"They don't have money on the chart," Cheryl said, consulting the card. "But it says that today is a triple-critical day for me."

"Then stay away from the slots."

"Are you kidding? Last time we went to Vegas I got three bars twice!"

"Play blackjack," he said, "the odds are better."

"Sure, the way *you* do it. If I could count cards, I'd walk away with a few thousand dollars every time, too."

"Even without counting," Rand said, "the game gives you better odds than the slots."

"I always do something wrong," she said. "I hit when I should stand, I stand when I should hit. . . ."

"Memorize the chart I gave you. It tells you exactly what to do."

"It's too hard," she said. "I can't memorize the chart. I'd rather play the slots."

"Well—at least stick around for the first hour or two to play for me. They know me in most places, but they don't know you yet."

"Do I have to play even on my honeymoon?"

"Of course," Rand said. "You don't want them to give me trouble, do you?"

They had a system. If Rand placed his chips to the left side of the circle, it meant Cheryl should hit. (Cheryl remembered this by thinking that if she was left back a grade, she was bad and should be hit.) The chips placed to the right meant she should stand and not take any cards. (She remembered this by thinking that when her answer was right, she would stand at the front of the class and everyone would applaud.) If Rand put his elbow on the table she was supposed to double down on her bet. If he reached into his pocket for his handkerchief, it meant she should bet a hundred dollars. If he took out his wallet and looked inside it, she was to bet *five hundred dollars.*

She felt important, having hundred-dollar chips on the table in front of her, and she loved it when he didn't make errors and they won big. Afterward he'd be so energetic and high, swinging her around in their room, making good love instead of letting her do all the work, later taking her to Spice on Ice, or some other flashy midnight show, both of them all dressed up. She adored the glitter — the massive headdresses, the pastel doves flying across the room, the seminude ice-skating — the glory and pageantry of it all. Rand wasn't interested in the dancers — even with their breasts hanging out of the costumes with cut-out fronts. He said he didn't think women marching around in circles on a stage were erotic. What he liked were the really dirty movies, which turned Cheryl on but made her feel slightly sick. She didn't need sick movies to be turned on, she was only nineteen and her blood pulsed at the slightest invitation, her dreams were lush with limbs and lips and loving whispers. But Rand said the movies were good for him; he needed to get a little charge now and then.

When she'd called home with the news, her mother had been hurt and angry. Cheryl was really surprised because her mother was tough and had always made fun of big affairs with strolling violinists and airplanes that flew by with flashing bulbs which spelled out "Congratulations on your marriage." She'd phoned from outside the Van Nuys courthouse to tell her parents she'd just been married, and her mother had said, "That's nice, I suppose," and then was absolutely silent. Cheryl almost said, You didn't really want to be there, did you? but thought better of it. Her mother didn't ask her a single question — like who was there, or what kind of ring he gave her, or which dress did she wear — so Cheryl finally volunteered into the silence that they were going to Las Vegas for their honeymoon.

"A work-play vacation?" her mother said. "How convenient for him."

"Can you put Daddy on?" Cheryl asked, wobbling in the phone booth on four-inch-high black heels. In the courthouse, she had turned her ankle coming up the stairs, wearing those heels. Rand liked her to wear that kind of shoe—he had bought her half a dozen pairs.

"Daddy's busy," her mother had said.

"Well—wish us luck," Cheryl said, wishing she didn't have to beg.

"In Vegas, . . . or for life?" her mother asked.

"Fuck it," Cheryl had answered, hanging up the phone. Maybe she hung up the phone first and then said it, she couldn't remember, with Rand standing there impatiently in his striped suit, his hair—still thick but at least half-gray—riffling in the breeze. She didn't bother to cry. Rand had no patience with her when she acted like a baby.

"Well, that takes care of your folks. They give you a bad time?" he asked, seeing her face.

"That's okay," she said, "it doesn't matter. Don't you want to call your son now?"

"Not really," Rand said.

"Well, he's the one that had a fit that we were living together."

"He'll find out," Rand said. "Let's just forget about them all right now and get this show on the road."

"Look what I got in the rest room of the coffee shop," Cheryl said as they drove along. "Mr. Hiram's Super Funbook with three free meals."

"Just what we need," Rand said. "Sirens in your ears, hookers bumping asses with you, and sexy Chinese girls patting the dollar slots, whispering 'Try this one, it's hot.' "

"At Mr. Hiram's they give you a free color photo," Cheryl said. "On one of our trips I went in there without you, and I got a picture of my face on a fake dollar bill, and a free phone call home."

"I can give you all the change you need," Rand said, "assuming you want to call home again."

"I don't. Believe me, I don't. But maybe it would be nice to get the free picture. Sort of a wedding picture."

"I've had enough of those already," Rand said. "Don't you think three is enough?"

"How about later on, maybe we can ask someone to take just one snapshot of us with my Polaroid?"

"Maybe," Rand said. "We'll see."

Cheryl stared for a while out the window at the spiky yucca plants and the knobby dwarfed trees. "I wonder if we'll have a room with a mirror this time," she said. "I wonder if we'll have fun."

"Don't we always?" Rand said.

Her best girlfriend had a job now doing word processing for ten dollars an hour. In high school they had talked about going on to junior college and studying computers, but in the end her friend got on-the-job training on a Wang and now worked in downtown LA for an engineering company.

Cheryl had taken a summer job at Saks, gift wrapping, and in the fall decided to stay with it a while until she had a clearer idea of what she wanted to do. Her mother and father seemed relieved that they weren't going to have to fork over five thousand a year to send her to some fancy college, and as long as she was paying her own gas and insurance on the '71 Ford they let her use, they didn't bother her. That is, until she met Rand — he was having a birthday present gift-wrapped for his third wife — and started seeing him every night. Then her parents started babbling all the usual stuff: "more than twice your age, after you because you're a gorgeous young girl, you ought to be dating his sons!"

What did they know? The guys her own age were nothing, invisible, scarecrows on hangers. They glugged beer and walked to some drumbeat in their heads; she was sick of faded jeans and running shoes and guys who couldn't wait to turn you on with grass or with their own throbbing bodies. They had no money, and never would. Times were getting so crazy that they all had to live with their parents, no one could afford the rent on an apartment, even sharing with two or three guys. Half of the guys she knew thought they would be famous rock stars; they couldn't even carry a tune.

Rand was a real person. He had a science degree, he had been an engineer or something for many years till he got sick of it. His kids, from his different wives, were all grown up, and he was sending his youngest son through college now. He really knew where it was at.

He never told dumb jokes. He didn't play games. He said what he wanted and she liked that. Do this, do that — and she did it, because usually it was a better idea than anything she could think of herself.

Now with their luggage carried in, he tipped the bellboy and locked the door of their room.

"Call room service and order us each a big shrimp cocktail," Rand said, his body reflected a dozen times in the mirrored room as he hung up his clothes in the alcove.

"I don't know if I want that," Cheryl said. "Maybe I want a hamburger."

"Call! Call!" he said. "Hurry up. When I get out of the shower I want it to be here."

And when it came, big white shrimp with pink tails and pink veins arched in a goblet over a snowball of ice, heads swimming in luscious red cocktail sauce, she knew he was right. It was exactly what she wanted. She chewed in a luxury of wanting the shrimp, grateful to him. When he came out of the shower she had eaten half of his shrimp, too — and he looked at the bloody plate and laughed, and peeled off his damp towel and swatted her. "That's what I love about you," he said. "Your healthy appetites. All of them."

By the time they got to the casino, she was quite satisfied, and chewed her lip comfortably while she adored him. She sat two stools down from him at the blackjack table, and felt his concentration burning toward her, his eyes counting the cards, figuring out when a ten-card would come up, knowing how many aces were left to fall at his — or the dealer's — place. The dealer was "Nancy from Indiana" — a sweet-faced, red-headed girl with heavy black eye makeup. He was joking with her, and tilting his toes, and counting cards at the same time. He was really brilliant. He won three forty-dollar bets in a row and bantered with the dealer: "It's not how you play the game, but whether you win or lose." The girl didn't get it. Cheryl hadn't gotten it the first time he'd said it either, but later he explained it to her and now she thought it was a funny joke. He took his handkerchief out of his pocket now, and Cheryl bet one hundred dollars on the next hand. It came up a ten and a jack, and she didn't even watch for his signal as he slid his chips to the right; she was catching on, she knew she had to stand with a twenty, it didn't matter what the dealer had. Bad luck! The dealer had blackjack. Nancy-from-Indiana swept the chips away, click, click, click, just like that, not caring for the narrowness of his eyes, the ugly clenching of his jaw muscles. This was what Cheryl hated, when it didn't go his way and his temper got foul.

She played the next three hands at his instruction, and twice he was wrong again. He had lost his concentration. He scooped up his remaining chips, raised an eyebrow at her, and walked to the keno lounge. After playing two token hands to establish that she was separate from him, in case the pit boss was watching, Cheryl met him there. He was adding some figures on a keno sheet, writing with thick black crayon.

"Why don't you ever play bingo with me?" she said. "I think that would be fun." The kind of look he gave her made her want to race away, to run all the way back to LA, to see her mother, even to go to junior college. She abruptly left him, saying she was going to the rest room.

A black woman in a uniform was mopping up leaks from the faucets with hotel towels. "You know how the engineers make these hotels," she said to Cheryl. "Every minute this place don't go up in flames, I thank God."

But the mirrors were perfect. They had the right kind of pink light coming down that always made her skin look especially creamy and smooth. She smiled at herself, a flash of a smile that was brilliant. Sometimes she really *was* gorgeous and she felt proud. When she stood at bus stops, her thick blonde hair blowing around her face, she impressed the traffic, she knew that.

"You winning, honey?" the black lady asked. Cheryl saw her white plate waiting, empty of tips.

"Yeah, I'm really lucky tonight," she said, digging in her big red nylon purse and putting a twenty-five-dollar chip on the plate. "This is my honeymoon."

"No kidding," the lady said. "How about that?"

Cheryl went out into the casino again, into the smoke and the clat-

ter of silver dollars and the raucous shouts coming from the craps
table. She saw Rand's rounded back hunched at another table; he
was playing again. She wandered around to the slot carousel, got
twenty silver dollars, and idly put them in a machine, three at a time,
to buy all three payoff lines. The last pull she only had two to put in,
and son of a gun, the three bars showed up on the bottom line and
she hadn't paid for them. Shit, she hated that. It happened once
before and she didn't get three hundred quarters. Things like that
could make her cry. She couldn't believe she would cry over something like that. Yet she was filling up, her nose and eyes, and she
wanted to say to God, How come not me? How come everyone else is
so lucky, only not me? Right next to her a young couple, maybe
twenty-two or twenty-three, had two ice buckets filled with silver
dollars. As she watched they hit another jackpot and the girl yelled,
"O-*kay!*" and the guy gave her a big hug. Cheryl checked to see if the
girl had a wedding ring. She did, and an engagement ring, too.
Cheryl looked at her own wedding band. Already she didn't like it;
she had picked the wrong one this morning. They had been in too
much of a hurry, trying to squeeze in a wedding and a trip to Vegas in
the same day. Rand had said he would buy her a diamond if they had
a big hit this weekend. The high rollers all bought their women jewelry. Sometimes the wives took half the winnings right off the table,
cashed in the chips, and went straight to the jewelry store to buy gold
bracelets. Cheryl would never have the nerve to scoop up half of
Rand's winnings. Maybe she just hadn't been married long enough.

    Now an old man on her other side hit three oranges and stood
back, chewing on a cigar, while thirty coins clanged down into the tin
bowl. He put three more dollars in the slot, and three bars turned up,
giving him a hundred more. He looked around for something to do
while the bells rang and the money arrived, and said to Cheryl, "You
using this machine?"

    "No, you can have it," she said, stepping back, and she felt a few
tears wash over the edge of her eye.

    "Hey, hey," the old man said. "You lose everything?"

    She nodded.

    "Then take a handful of mine. Go ahead, I won't feel it. I have oil
wells."

"I don't think so," Cheryl said. "I have to quit now."

"Here," he insisted. "Just fill up a bucket."

"It doesn't work that way," Cheryl said. "I don't think you can use someone else's luck." She went out to the lobby to look at the waterfall. A new bride was standing there, a young Mexican girl with flowers on her wrist. Her husband, a handsome Latino with a pencil mustache, wearing a white jacket, came over to Cheryl and said, "Could you take a picture of us, please?" He handed her his camera. "Just push here."

They were both children, Cheryl thought. Men her own age were really children, weren't they? She took a picture they would keep forever, but they would never remember her standing there, taking it. She knew she would always remember them.

"We appreciate it," the girl said, the water crashing down behind her, sending up a rainbow spray of dots against the rocks. To their retreating backs Cheryl said, "I wish I had a wedding picture. I just got married, too."

Deciding to go back to the hotel room, she crossed the pool area and saw a Hawaiian luau in progress. Four black-haired girls in flowered red dresses were dancing a hula on a wooden platform. The music was very serene and dreamy; the girls' hands were as delicate as birds. Their hips slid slowly back and forth under their long dresses as if they were under water. Cheryl knew she would never be that peaceful. She stood on the damp grass and watched, feeling the tears come again. Then she took the elevator up to their room and fell asleep.

"Butterflies, Love-Lites, roses, cigars. . . ." The cigar girl passed their table in the coffee shop and Cheryl tapped her on the back. The girl swung around, her long stockinged legs seeming to take up most of her body.

"Are those Love-Lites you're wearing?" Cheryl asked. "How do they work?" The girl wore flashing red lantern earrings, a blinking red pendant, and a blinking butterfly pin.

"Little hearing-aid batteries," the girl said. "They last forever."

"Could you get me one, Rand?" Cheryl asked, smiling at him.

"Sure," he said. He was composed again, shaved and smelling of Brut. "If you like. . . ." He took out his wallet. "How much?"

"Twenty-five," the girl said, "if you want the Love-Lite earrings." Cheryl imagined that if she were ever in a dark tunnel, the Love-Lites would light her way to safety. She took off her little ivory elephant earrings and attached the new ones to her ears.

They finished eating their breakfast. She and Rand were in the hotel with a huge gold-colored pot outside—about fifty feet high with a fake ugly rainbow coming up to it.

"Cheap," Cheryl had remarked as they turned into the parking lot. "It makes the whole idea cheap. Now whenever I see a rainbow I'll be reminded of this brassy pot and this ugly rainbow. And when I hear 'Over the Rainbow' I'll think of smoky rooms and bad bets."

"Maybe you'll think of mirrored rooms and piles of money."

"Same thing," Cheryl said.

"Well, let's get going. I could use you to play for me this morning."

"I don't really want to," she said. "I want to do something else. You're safe. They don't know you here, do they? It's a new hotel."

"I suppose I could get along without you for a while. But not tonight."

"I'll play for you tonight, then."

"And do what all day?"

"Who knows?" she said. "Go to Hoover Dam maybe."

As soon as she got on the tour bus she felt a little better. The casinos always seemed like churches to her, with people praying for grace all over the place. You could feel it when you passed a bingo room, the hush, the living prayer, as they all waited to be chosen. In Vegas, to pray and to play was the same thing: you could get saved, you could get lucky. Only the difference was, if God gave you grace, no one lost. In Vegas, if you won, you were just ruining the next guy.

Cheryl leaned her face into the air-conditioning slit under the window. The bus was filling up with lots of elderly ladies. She never wanted to be one of them, with their bluish hair and their pointy eyeglasses. They looked like old birds, all the same. How did they ever have any fun? Sometimes Rand looked like an old bird with his skinny shins, the way the skin on his legs seemed scaly. She was glad he was cooped up in some casino, in the dark daytime inside of those places. She was going out into the sun . . . where she could thaw out. She was definitely feeling better. She looked out the window as the bus crossed the desert and she decided there *was* scenery out there. She saw pinkish clay rock formations, and long sandy stretches of browns and beiges and pinks. It looked like a painting. Some clouds were lining up overhead, so it didn't seem quite as hot or bright. Sometimes she thought she had seen everything, thought everything she was ever going to see or think, and the next eighty years of her life were going to be exactly the same as the first twenty. But once in a while she saw something new and got a different feeling, and when that happened, it gave her hope again. At first, being with Rand had given her a thousand new thoughts and feelings, but now she was having no new ones. Like everything else, it had gotten old—and she had only married him yesterday. If, as her mother said, the marriage —considering his record—was sure to be a short-term thing, then *that* was rotten. And if it was to be forever, till death did they part, that seemed rotten, too.

When she first started living with Rand, her mother had said, "Just don't come back home to us with a baby for me to take care of for you." It never occurred to her that she might have a baby with Rand. One of his sons' wives was pregnant. He didn't seem like the type of husband you'd want to have a baby with, a man who already was going to be a grandfather.

"Hoover Dam up ahead," the bus driver announced. "When we park, please line up at the second tower on the Nevada side."

As soon as she got out of the bus, Cheryl found herself behind a young couple in black motorcycle jackets. They each had one hand stuck in the butt pocket of the other's jeans. The girl, curvy and very cute, had long fuzzy black hair, while the guy was tall and good-looking, and wore pointy lizard-skin boots. Cheryl admired his dark wavy hair. When he turned to look down at the river, Cheryl saw a toothpick in his mouth. He made her heart leap, giving out that kind of raw sexiness that did something to her. She wished she were his girl. For a minute, she would have given anything to be that girl.

Blocks of tourists, maybe twenty at a time, were allowed to board the elevator. For five minutes at a time the line came to a stop. Every time it stopped, the guy took the toothpick out of his mouth and kissed his girl, bending her backward passionately. Once the girl looked behind her, embarrassed, and smiled apologetically at Cheryl.

"That's okay," Cheryl said, "I don't mind. I think love is great." She walked behind them as they inched toward the elevator, and looked down the vast sloping side of the dam, which curved downward to the Colorado River, a greenish strip far below them. Tiny dots—birds—flew and lifted against the concrete curve. Cheryl realized that a person could easily kill himself by jumping off here. She had also noticed that it would be easy from the parking garage of The Mint, seventh level, and filed away the information in her head. Most public places tried to keep you from killing yourself, putting up high fences or barbed wire, but then there were other places that didn't seem to worry about the possibility. Right here, at Hoover Dam, you could just get up on the waist-high railing and jump down into the curving concrete side of the dam. If she ever really needed to do it, it would be a long ride from LA.

The motorcycle couple moved along with the line. Now the guy, wearing a black T-shirt under his leather jacket with the words "Harley Davidson, Denver, Colo, USA" on it, had his hand under his girl's belt line and was pressing down to bare skin, as far as he could get under the tight jeans.

"Hey," the girl whispered to him, peeking over her shoulder at Cheryl, "don't do that." The guy turned around and winked at Cheryl. "Hey, you come here too, sweetheart. I have two hands; I can do you both at once." Cheryl laughed and took a step forward, and then the guy had his arm around her, too. The girl laughed and he laughed and the line began to move forward quickly, so she crowded into the elevator with them, and the three of them descended into the mountain, 528 feet down, clinging together.

They walked through a long tiled tunnel behind their guide, a short man with a booming voice who assured them the tunnel did not leak. It was cold in the tunnel and the lights above them were very dim. Now and then the bulbs would black out for a few seconds. Cheryl could feel the thrumming vibration of machinery all around her. "The walls of the dam are 107 feet thick," the guide said. "It is

726 feet high." She was still wrapped in the arm of the guy in the motorcycle jacket. "If you've heard rumors that men were trapped in the concrete, put your minds at ease. The cement here was poured eighteen inches at a time, so it could cure, and you can't lose a man in eighteen inches of concrete. *However,* it *is* true that ninety-six workers were killed between 1931 and 1937: twenty-four fell to their deaths, three drowned, ten were killed by explosions, five were electrocuted, twenty-six were struck by falling debris, twenty-six were struck by machinery, one died in the elevator, and one in a cableway accident."

The girl who was sharing her guy with Cheryl shivered. "How creepy," she said. "What if we get stuck down here?"

"Don't worry," Cheryl offered. "I have my Love-Lites." She held back her hair and showed the girl the glowing lanterns swinging from her ears. "If anything goes wrong, they'll light our way out of here." The girl reached over and took her hand tightly. "How neat," she said. "We're so lucky to have you. This place spooks me."

Cheryl changed places with the guy so that she was between him and the girl; she held hands with both of them going down the long tunnel. In the powerhouse they saw the row of immense electric generators which took the river water and turned it into electricity. The guide gave them a thousand figures, and while he told them how many acres the lake covered, how many kilowatts the power plant produced, Cheryl noticed some little metal machines that resembled robots, funny round tubs with bleeping antennae. She pointed them out to the girl, who squeezed her hand tighter and giggled. "This is so much fun," she said. "I'm so glad we found you."

"Want me to take a picture of you two with my Polaroid?" Cheryl asked, hunting in her nylon bag for her camera. They were being led now through a diversion tunnel, a long dark passage made of volcanic rock ten to fifteen million years old, through which water had run while the dam was being built. The three of them let the tour group pass by them, and then stood alone in the black tunnel. The rocky sides dripped moisture from condensation, and as in a subway train, the lights flickered and went out. From far down the passageway they could hear the gasps and delighted fright of the tourists, and the guide's reassuring voice. Cheryl stood secure in the pinkish glow of her Love-Lites, her new friends gathered close to her. She arranged them against the jagged wall and let her flash explode.

"Want us to take a picture of you?" the girl asked.

"That would be real nice," Cheryl said. "This is sort of a special occasion for me—I've been wishing someone would take a picture of me all day."

"Couldn't you ask anyone?" the girl said.

"Not really," Cheryl said. "I'm out here by myself." Just as she tore the finished picture from the camera and handed it over to them, the lights flashed on, illuminating the three of them in a ring of whiteness. "Look," she said to the guy, "I even got your boots in the picture."

He laughed. "I guess you know what counts," he said. "Here, let me take you now." He posed her against the rock, and she tossed her hair back to let her lanterns shine out. While they were waiting for the print, her friends told Cheryl that they were staying in a camper parked at some strip hotel, and were heading for Zion in the morning.

"Say," the guy said, "if you're traveling alone, maybe you'd like to come along with us for a while." He put his hand on his girl's shoulder and said, "How's that for an idea?"

The girl looked at him. "Well, I guess we could squeeze her in."

"Sure," he said, "the more the merrier."

Cheryl, her back against the rough wall, felt as if the gates of the dam had just been opened, and she was being swept out to sea on the emerald waters.

"Will you do it?" he asked. The girl had taken out an Afro comb and was picking at her fuzzy curls, standing a little away from them.

"Yeah . . . sure. I will! It sounds great."

"Where are you staying?" he asked. "We'll have to come by and get your luggage."

But just then there was a last warning call for the elevator going up, and because she couldn't run fast on her high heels, they got way ahead of her making a dash down the tunnel. Dancing with impatience, Cheryl had to wait for the second trip up. When she got to the surface they were gone. She walked frantically from the tower on the Nevada side to the tower on the Arizona side, and searched for them in the crowd near the statues of the Winged Figures of the Republic at the entrance to the dam. She heard a faint buzz reverberating off the canyon walls, and in the distance saw the little ant of their motorcycle climbing the hairpin road toward the desert.

Finally she joined the crowd of old ladies going back to the tour bus, and when she found a seat she settled down to study her wedding picture. It was just her luck, she thought, that even the Love-Lites didn't shine out in it. They hung there, like charred corks, from her ears.

At the Fence

She is standing on her neighbors' doorstep, seeing herself as they will see her in a second: a cranky, middle-aged lady with a complaint. For an instant she is *them* seeing herself come up the walk in a polyester dress, her hair going gray, peering into their screen door, into their private life, prepared to introduce some petty irritation into their newlywed bliss.

She can see the young man lounging on the floor, his back against the couch cushions, watching the end of the Yankee-Dodger game. He has just come home from work and is drinking a beer. At first she thinks he might be wearing his underwear, but sees with relief as she puts her eyes to the screen that his shorts are of the jogging or swimsuit variety. His wife is in the kitchen, heating another frozen pizza. Anna believes — because of the nightly odor of oregano and sizzling mushrooms — that the young couple must eat pizza for every dinner during the week; on weekends it must be steak because then Anna can smell the fire-starter burning on their outdoor barbecue grill.

"Uh, yes?" the young man answers to her unwelcome knock, getting up reluctantly and glancing back at the TV screen. He shakes a long lock of black hair out of his eyes.

"Excuse me," Anna says, "I'm sorry to bother you, but I'm your neighbor, Mrs. Mazer, I live next door, and your dog was barking as he often does till after two o'clock in the morning. He has a very loud bark."

The young man looks behind him, and there comes the dog — a

sleek black Doberman trotting right to the door, his long snout coming up against the screen, his stubby tail wagging.

"Yeah, he does, doesn't he?" the young man says, and bends protectively to pet his dog.

To show her good will, Anna says sincerely, "He's really a beautiful animal." Just then the man's wife swings into view, wiping her hands on her blue jeans. She is perhaps a year or two younger than her husband, about nineteen, the age of Anna's oldest daughter, Karen, yet she comes to the door as if she owns not only this rented house, but also the world with Anna in it. She puts her hand on her husband's bare shoulder; only then is Anna aware of the thick black hair on his chest, the private hole of his navel looking at her eye. The girl has cornsilk blonde hair, long and thick, and she twists it, rope-like, over one shoulder as she stands there looking out. Her breasts are heavy and loose inside a blue T-shirt.

"Hi, I'm Liz," she says conversationally.

"The dog—" Anna continues. "I realize it's a new place for him here, but I would like you to be aware that he whines and howls all day when you're both at work, and last night—I guess you were out late—he was really frantic, running from one end of the yard to the other, barking hysterically. Even if you *are* home he tends to bark in the middle of the night, but it's worse when you're gone. I guess he stopped barking when you came home, around two."

"Yeah," he says, "that's when we came home, around two."

Anna wonders where they went, and what could be more enticing than this new little house, their bedroom at the back with a glass door to the garden, the kitchen so handy to warm up frozen foods in. The husband looks over his shoulder at the TV.

"I don't mean to disturb you, really," Anna says, "but it's agonizing to be trying to sleep and to have that bark never stopping. It makes me feel desperate, as if I have no control over my life."

Too melodramatic, I'm telling them too much, she thinks, moving away from the screen and down a step, to show she is going, won't take any more of their time.

"Yeah, well, we hope he quiets down." He scratches his thigh, and adds, "But he's not going to be sleeping in the house—we got a new rug."

"Look — " Anna says, suddenly thinking of how her heart pounded last night as she listened to that piercing, perpetual racket and of how she considered calling the police, then realized they could do nothing more than some official preliminary paperwork, "the thing is I work at home, I do calligraphy, and I often work outside on the patio, or in my bedroom, and I just can't concentrate with all that noise. Even when it's quiet, I know he's going to start in a minute again, or *could,* and I just can't function." To her surprise, she hears her voice crack and feels tears heat her eyes. She didn't know she could act this well; at least she thinks she's acting because she didn't know she felt this badly.

The young man is bored now. She can see him wondering how this crying woman got here just when the Dodgers were going up to bat. But she can't leave without saying just a few more things. "The point is, I can't *do* anything to control what's happening to me," she begs in spite of herself. "I can't stop your dog from barking and there's no room in my house where I can hide. I hear him *everywhere* — even in the closet! If only I could contact you during the day to tell you about it! It's been going on for a whole month now, since the day you moved in."

"Well, I guess he's lonely," the wife says suddenly. "What he needs is another dog to play with." She snickers. "But *it'd* probably bark, too."

"I don't understand why you have a pet, just to leave him alone all day. Why do you need a dog? You both work!"

"Hey!" the husband says with a flare of anger. "That's *why* he's here. I mean, if we were both here all day, why would we need a watchdog?"

"Well, I'm home all day," Anna says, backtracking with a weak smile, believing for an instant she can convince them to give their dog away and make her their watchdog. "I could watch out for you. I mean, I always look out my windows. If I saw anything funny going on, if I saw a truck in your driveway, I could call you. Is there someplace I could reach you during the day?"

Her voice is reedy with guile: she really wants to be able to call them up and scream, "Come home and shut him up! I can't listen to that noise another second!"

"If she saw a truck in the driveway," the wife says, "it'd probably be one of your buddies." She elbows her husband and laughs.

"Well, me," he says, keeping to the point. "I'm a housepainter, so I can't be reached, and she—well, she works in a store and you can't call her there." His voice is protective and mean now, he's had enough of this, and to show it he bends down and pats the dog again, lovingly. "Good boy, Fletch, yeah, we'll get you some of that good food soon."

Anna feels worse than she did in the middle of the night. It's gone wrong. The young man is really hostile now, and she's gotten nowhere, just a crank on his doorstep.

"You know, I like animals, I really love them," Anna says in a last effort to set it right, show them that she's a fair, nice person. "I mean, I'm all for pets. I have two cats myself—."

"Yeah," he says. "*They're* probably what makes my dog bark. One of them was in my yard. I even fed it. I sure won't do *that* again." Now he's holding the dog by its red leather collar as if to keep it from springing at her throat. She suddenly remembers a half-dozen movies in which Dobermans were killers, one in which Rock Hudson is a mad scientist who discovers a way to age a human embryo to an old woman in a few short weeks. Anna thinks that it was just yesterday she was newly married, and now she's old. She doesn't believe the problems she's thinking about these days could really be her problems. She hasn't had enough of starting out, she's just getting used to being grownup, being married.

"We also have a little aviary—maybe you've seen my daughter's birds when your dog gets out the door and you come up between the houses to get him."

"He don't ever get out," the husband says threateningly, stepping back, his hand on the door now, ready to close it on her.

"But he does!" Anna says. "You were in my yard just yesterday morning."

"Not me," he says. "Sorry—we got to eat now," and he closes the door.

Anna's husband is doing a crossword puzzle at the kitchen table;

her oldest daughter has her book bag over her shoulder and the keys to Anna's car in her hand.

"I'm going over to Ben's," she says. "See you—."

Anna wants to ask, Aren't you going to have dinner with us? When will you be home? Do you have a sweater? but those are old records that spin soundlessly around her children's ears.

"What if *I* need to use my car?" she says instead, meanly, striking a bull's-eye.

"Do you?" Karen asks.

"No, I don't," Anna says, "but what if I did?"

"Then Ben would come and get me," Karen says reasonably.

"On his motorcycle," Anna says. "Well. . . go"—waving her away—"go see Ben."

Ben, her daughter's lover, is the wrong man for her daughter, but Karen says she will marry him very soon. Not *live* with him, which Anna often prays will happen, but *marry* him. Anna would much prefer the new arrangement for them so when Karen grows up and finds out how off-center he is, how insincere, superficial, humorless, stupid, the break won't be as complex as divorce. Anna also reasons that if Karen moved in with Ben, she would be out of her way, out of the house where now Anna has to witness her in her adolescent turbulence, its ugly, heavy, despairing side. She doesn't even want to look up from her desk these days when Karen comes in sullenly from classes at the junior college, doesn't want to say, How was school? as she said it, gladly, when Karen (bright and darling and lovable) was in second grade but going daily to do reading with the sixth graders. Karen has given notice that she is going to quit school to get a job so she can marry Ben. Ben has no plans, no interests right now, and even that isn't the trouble. It isn't his motorcycle, either—Anna is not that dense or backward. It's just that her heart hurts when she considers Karen's giving her life to that dull boy, a boy who makes rat-tat-tat sounds like a six-year-old playing soldier whenever he describes some fantasy film he's seen in which lasers shoot out of spacecrafts.

As she sets dinner plates on the table, her husband, Lou, absently raises the newspaper to let her get one under it. *His* mother was convinced Anna was the wrong girl for *him* more than twenty years ago, and she fought Anna like a banshee, with threats, scenes, blackmail, insults, curses. To no avail, of course—here they are, not having half the fun his mother was afraid they were going to have, and not anywhere as ruined as his mother predicted. But ruined enough, by normal attrition, repetition, the insidious deadening of responses. At least at the beginning there was that spark arcing over them, between them, encircling them, which clearly Karen has not got with Ben— there *is* no current as far as Anna can see, but Karen, in her dullness, doesn't even seem to know there's that to hope for.

The other children, old teenagers, come dragging into the kitchen for dinner; they used to set the table for her, used to check a wheelchart on the refrigerator for their weekly chores, used to vacuum, straighten up the bathroom, take out the garbage. Now they do nothing but wait to be waited on, and Anna hasn't the strength to fight back anymore. Arguing takes more energy than doing everything herself, though her energy level, in general, is very low, and losing sleep every night hasn't helped.

"That black dog," she says to Lou, "you heard him last night, didn't you?"

"Well, yeah, I suppose, maybe I did."

"Don't say that just for my sake," Anna says. "Did you hear that horrible barking or didn't you?"

"I think I was sleeping," Lou says.

God, she thinks, *heavy and impenetrable, like his daughter Karen. Hardly conscious sometimes.* Maybe if his mother had tried just a little harder, Anna would have been saved from him, from this life of servicing him and his children. Sometimes she says it aloud, that she doesn't feel she has her own life, and Lou or one of the children will say complacently, "Well, you have your calligraphy."

But she can't even do her calligraphy with the dog howling. Sometimes a distant fire engine or police siren will start the dog going, and he begins a thin wailing, less eerie than the coyotes' wailing she hears at night from the hills, but burdened enough, an outward-spiraling tornado of loneliness and misery. Then it will pause briefly before turning into an explosion of staccato barks, getting shriller and more panicky, till finally the animal is running from one end of the yard to the other, rattling the fence, clawing at the spaces between the boards, yipping and yapping in a frenzy that can go on, easily, for several hours without pause.

"They should require every person who owns a dog to have the dog's larynx removed," Anna says, dropping silverware onto the table. "No one has a right to do this, to destroy a person's peace, just because he likes the idea of having a dog. A man and his dog! — what a dumb, romantic notion."

At the same moment she is thinking that she would like Karen to marry a young man like the one next door. A man who has a dog — a man, who, with his woman and his beer and his ballgame, seems like the sort of man a woman should have, a man who protects his rights, who doesn't back down, who stands firm. She thinks of his hairy chest, and to her surprise something clutches low down in her abdomen, in the place where the estrogen is running low.

She wishes all her children would move out tomorrow and end it right there. She wishes Lou were really her father and she could live in the house with him but still go out in the world for adventure and romance, and then he'd be there to hold her warmly when she came in from her excursions in the shimmering night world.

Of course, it could never happen. Sometimes she feels she will never go anywhere again, and if she does, it won't matter where, she'll be bored and tired at any spot in the universe. As far as her success as a mother goes, if she has raised such a perfect child, her first-born, Karen, who knew the names of all the dinosaurs at three, how come a girl like that dopey blonde next door can figure out how to set up such a neat arrangement for herself, a handsome man, a bed, an endless supply of pizzas, while Karen falls in with a young man of no redeeming charm or beauty or intelligence whatsoever? Do all parents feel this about their children? Is it her duty to intervene and *forbid*? or at least try to? At first she thought interfering was against her principles, but now she realizes she just hasn't the energy to do it. What difference can it make? In the end she will have to recognize that her children aren't perfect people, no matter how much of herself she handed over to them — they're just ordinary, mixed-up kids who have all the predictable problems.

Besides, how can she know if her instincts are correct? What if she insists that Karen never see Ben again...and then Karen never in her life meets another man who wants her? Then she'll live forever with Lou and Anna — she'll be a spinster of fifty and Lou and Anna will be seventy-five, and she'll be taking Anna's car out to the cotton-spool factory where her job will be to spin cotton onto plastic spools. Who will do Karen's laundry when Anna and Lou have died? No one; she'll never wear clean underpants again, and won't care, either.

It's getting away from her. Anna serves dinner. Later, when she goes to bed, she watches the cold computerized numbers of the digital clock and thinks how buttons are taking over the world, video games and phones and microwave ovens and food processors and word processors and machines on which you can play carnal movies in your bedroom. Warmth has gone out of everything. She shivers with a chill, and at that moment the dog starts to bark and her body flares with anger or sorrow or with a vindictive hormonal flush, and then she feels as if she is burning in hell.

Judge, she says to herself, getting her case in order, *do you think it's fair? Don't dogs belong in big country spaces where they can roam and explore? Isn't it a true crime to lock an animal in a yard and then leave it alone all day, and long into the night? And isn't my home my castle? Shouldn't I be able to take a nap, or read a book, or make love* (as long as we're envisioning the ideal life) *without either the threat of sudden barking or its actual occurrence? Is there no way justice can be done in my favor?*

She will not tell the judge her other fantasies: how the young couple shake the little house with the force of their passion (a young wife does not have soft swinging breasts for nothing), how, after the beer and the pizza and the ballgame, the young man takes his other satisfactions before he has to go out into the cold morning world to smooth fresh new paint over old walls.

And is it the appearance of this dog in her life which is really the greatest injustice that has been done to her? And what about the moral wrong done to the black dog with his long moist snout as he daily runs from one end of the yard to the other — hardly a watchdog, hardly a man's best friend, just a whimpering, crazed abandoned creature, without a mate, without a friend.

On the next weekend night, long after the coals in the barbecue grill on the other side of the fence have died out and the couple has roared away in their pickup truck, when the full moon is overhead, Anna gets her two biggest pot covers and takes them out into the backyard. She holds them poised like a cymbal player waiting for her cue in the pit of a great orchestra. In the house her remaining daughters are sprawled on unchanged bedsheets, sleeping in old sweatshirts and torn cords. Karen has not come home from Ben's yet —she often does not arrive till three or four o'clock in the morning. Lou is posed in bed like a marble statue on a sarcophagus. On Anna's desk are a hundred blank sheets of beige bond paper on which she is to hand-letter wedding invitations for a high school friend of Karen's, a girl who is marrying a twenty-seven-year-old astronomer, handsome and highly placed in a government job.

Anna waits, counting the beats, as breathless as if the stars are her vast audience and this is her debut. And when it comes, first the whine, then the howl, then the full-fledged bass and treble of the mad dog's great range, she runs in her nightgown, barefoot, across the damp grass of the yard, runs to the fence and crashes the pot covers together in a series of clashes, bangs and shrieks till the night sky shakes with the lightening and thunder of her fury.

Then. . .silence. She has terrified him. She feels her lip curl. Hah, good. She imagines the dog to be like a native in the jungle who witnesses a meteorite fall. He will be cowering now under the oleanders, his ordinary restless anguish changed to full terror. Well, this is only the beginning. She will teach him.

Back in the house, she sees that she has actually awakened her sleeping daughters. They are stumbling, bleary-eyed, down the hall. What happened, they wonder. A car crash? Only her husband still sleeps: no kiss, no catastrophe, no symphony can wake him.

Anna replaces the pot covers in the cabinet under the stove, but not before a sliver of silver metal, shredded from the edge of one of the covers by her wild banging, pierces her finger, drawing bright blood.

The next day she buys a pair of ear plugs, little cylinders of wax and foam, and at night jams them into her ears as if she is corking up her vital fluids. After she inserts them and lies down under the covers she hears only the pounding of her heart, each beat pushing the ear plugs, little by little, out of her, as when her husband, that last, long-ago time, fell asleep during lovemaking and in slow pulsing degrees slipped from her body.

She tries to sink down to sleep, but now anxieties of what she cannot hear reach her consciousness — the phone (her old mother, stricken, or Karen on the night streets in the old car, stranded, raped); the creaking of a door (a burglar); the whispering of passionate noises in her ear by her husband (he is not ninety; he is only facing in his way what she is facing in hers).

But then, as though through deep water, the dog's barking reaches her mind, blurred but stirring, a call to her energies: she is needed out there at the fence, she is wanted. This time she carries the tape recorder into the yard and carefully, like a technician fully versed in the uses of the buttons of destruction, presses "RECORD," gathering evidence for the judge in her case against the young couple, those lucky folks, so obliviously licking oregano from each other's lips, or peacefully, deeply sleeping.

The next day she writes the newlyweds a letter on a piece of the beige wedding-invitation stationery, taking a risk. Her daughter's friend probably will not count them, will never know Anna has only sold them ninety-nine sheets and taken pay for one hundred.

Dear Neighbors—[she writes in her best italic script]—
I am not well due to the barking of your dog. Please
put him in the house or take him with you wherever you go.
You have brought chaos into my life by moving to this quiet

*block, and I will have no recourse but to call the police
if you do not take proper measures.*

Anna Mazer

It has taken her almost thirty minutes to write this, using her finest, most graceful golden nib. She ought to send them a bill for her services. They probably have more money than she has — after all, they eat steak, which Anna never buys, and they haven't got three sullen children to buy clothes and educations for. *Someone* ought to pay her!

Making sure they have left for work (both cars gone), she strides out past her walk and along the street to their mailbox, where she leaves the letter. Then, thinking better of it, she takes it out and carries it by hand to their kitchen door, where they enter every night after the day's work. She slides it under the door. As she does so, the dog comes trotting into view from the backyard, and she is within a foot of him as he pushes his snout against the space between the boards in the side gate.

It occurs to her that she will poison the dog if his owners don't fix up the trouble in her life. The dog yips, and absently she pats him through the fence as she plans what she will do. Valium in a hot dog, perhaps. But it probably won't kill, just sedate. If necessary she will go into the city and find a real drug pusher on a street corner. (She could probably ask Ben; no doubt he would know the right people.) A calculated number of barbiturates would do it. She wishes she were more knowledgeable in this seamier side of life.

The dog is licking her hand, dancing with pleasure at her company, his rear end wiggling in rippling convulsions. No one has been that happy to see her in a long time. She kneels and begins to croon to him, "You hate them for the way they leave you alone, and *I* hate them for the way they leave you alone. We should join forces, you know. Why don't you kill them, like the dog tries to do in the Rock Hudson movie?" She laughs. This is all very silly. She feels suddenly happy, not having laughed in some time.

"So long, kid," she says to the dog. "Try to have a nice day. Try meditation. Don't get so tense about everything."

Back in her house, she sits down at her desk and begins work on the wedding invitations. If Karen were to marry Ben, would she have to be personally responsible for a big party? For wedding invitations, dinners, a band, liquor? Would she have to make hors d'oeuvres and pass them around on little trays to Ben's friends who are wearing Star Trek T-shirts?

His parents are divorced and living on different continents. She thinks of his short stubby fingers and his brash thighs, riding her daughter. Perhaps — who knows about such things? — even sluggish, dull daughters might feel something.

When the dog begins to cry, she goes out in the yard and gives him a hot dog through the fence — to get him used to the idea, she tells herself, but he comes so fast to the fence, looks at her with his liquid brown eyes so longingly, that she feels her heart leap with gladness. She goes back into the house and brings out the whole package of hot dogs, feeding them to him one by one, watching with satisfaction as he devours them with pleasure.

Yet late that night, when the barking begins just as she has fallen asleep, she flails out in frustration, groaning, and strikes her husband in the center of his soft stomach.

"What? What?" he says, sitting bolt upright, and then he hears the sound. "The dog again, eh?" he says. "Are they home?"

"They don't hear *anything*," Anna says.

"Well, now *I* hear it." He looks to his wife for approval; finally now, after so long, he hears it. He once again has something in common with her.

"What do you want me to do?" he asks. "Call them?"

"Why don't you?" Anna says. She feels suddenly excited, her husband is going to stand up for her, like the young man with the beer and the dog stands up for *his* wife, doesn't let anyone call her at work.

"Look up their number," he says, but she already is pushing buttons on the bedside phone; she has known their number by heart from the beginning. The digital clock reads 3:33. When her husband takes the phone from her as it begins to ring, she dashes into the kitchen and lifts the extension.

"Hullo?" finally comes the dull voice of the young man, heavy with sleep or sex. She can imagine him standing somewhere in that honeymoon cottage, naked, hairy, hot with the beating of his young blood.

"This is your neighbor," her husband says in a deep voice. "We're having trouble sleeping because of your dog. Could you do something about it?"

"God damn!" the young husband says. "Get the fuck off our backs, will you? We don't want fancy letters from your wife, either. You're just a couple of fucking old farts,"—and Anna hears him hang up the phone.

She comes back to the bedroom, her face flushed, her blood pounding in her head. Already her husband is calling the police, his anger causing his fingers to tremble as they search among the buttons. She listens while he tells the police the story, gives the address, hangs up. "They're coming over to talk to the guy," her husband says. "I won't be treated that way. I'll go to court! If necessary I'll go over there and kill it!"

Kill it. For her. She is overwhelmed. She turns the lamp off and gets into bed beside her husband. She embraces him, turning on her side toward his stretched-out body. They lay tensely, waiting for the lights of the police car, which finally come washing up over the ceiling.

They can hear the policeman knocking on the front door of the little house next door. There is a low interchange of polite voices. Her interests are being protected, she is going to be taken care of. They hear the door close, the police car backing out of the driveway, driving away.

"Well, maybe now we can get some sleep." Her husband pats her shoulder, moves her arm off his stomach, and seems instantly to be breathing softly, drifting into sound sleep. All the breath goes out of her. Now she is filled with fear. The young man is the type who probably has a gun in his house. A real man has a dog and a gun. He will blast her children in the yard. Or strangle her cats. Or slash the aviary wire and let out her daughter's precious birds—she can see the flutter of finches and doves as they ascend over the house and fly away forever. It will end as a headline in a tabloid newspaper. Her husband will kill the black Doberman with his bare hands and the young man will get out his gun and shoot her husband. Karen will marry Ben. Her other daughters will run off to a commune. The wind will blow away her wedding invitations, and the ink will come out of her pen nib in blots.

She imagines the young man right now stroking the polished barrel of his shotgun, and she feels herself arc out of bed and land on her toes like a ballet dancer. She hurries into the backyard. The stars are as sharp as at the beginning of creation. A tall palm at the far end of the yard is fanned out against the moon. There is a rustling in the brush on the other side of the fence as she approaches it.

She whispers, "Here boy, come here," and the beautiful black dog with his princely face comes to the fence and thrusts his warm nose through the crack till it is cupped in her fingers.

"Listen. . ." she says. "Just wait here and be very quiet." She walks on the sharp, damp blades of grass to the door at the back of the garage and returns with a hammer. By the light of the moon she pulls and pries at a board in the fence until she wrenches it from the bottom rail. Making a tiny kissing sound with her lips she holds it aside and the dog pours through like a waterfall, shimmering and coursing down the length of her leg. She kneels and puts both arms around him, long enough to feel his hot breath on her face.

"Come with me," she says, standing and leading him by his red collar up the patio steps, into the house, and across the soft carpeting of the living room. He follows her out the front door and into the wide street where they both stand in silence, panting in the cool air. His ears are up, his hind legs spread slightly apart. She bends quickly and gives him a sharp rap on his rump.

"Go!" she commands. "Go!"

He starts forward like a thoroughbred, like a whippet, a black arrow flying into the dewy night. She watches him gallop till his image begins to fade against the slurry blacktop. She doesn't breathe as she sees him pause, tense, and then leap in a single bound over the horizon. At that moment she realizes she has forgotten to climb upon his back.

Straight from the Deathbed

Her son, Will, when he was a baby, had had such a heavy head that Edna worried for years that he wouldn't grow up right. She watched from behind the drapes of her apartment as Will, his wife, Martha, and their daughter Eileen took their suitcases out of the station wagon. They had driven up to see her from Los Angeles, an eight-hour trip. Will was a schoolteacher now, and had been for the past twenty-five years, so there was nothing wrong with his head, but it was still huge, and Edna didn't look forward to seeing the blank, watery look in his eyes. Only Martha could snap him out of it; from the time he was seventeen she was the only one who could hold his attention. She had been such an ugly, puny girl then. *No one* could have imagined twenty-five years ago that she would turn out to be a prize.

There was no point in feeling guilty, though. Edna let the drape fall into place and waited on her toes for the buzzer on the wall to ring. She wasn't sorry then and she wasn't going to be sorry now for the commotion she and Harry had made about that girl; how could they have known she would turn out so capable, so much more sensible than Will, and much better natured (although not that much at first, due to their strained relations). If her husband, Harry, had known then — on the day he threw Martha out of their house and told her never to come back — if he had known then what brilliant children the girl would bear and raise, if he had known what pride he would take in his grandchildren, he would have apologized on bended knee to her for what he had done on that day after she and Will announced their engagement.

It wasn't till Harry was clearly on his deathbed that he felt the necessity of making an apology. He had told Edna to draw the curtains around his bed and put her ear right against his dry lips. What a production he wanted! Edna had to promise to deliver his apology publicly to his wronged daughter-in-law on the day of his funeral. He had the script all planned out; he wanted a cantor to sing "The Impossible Dream" and he wanted Edna to go up and stand with the rabbi and make a public statement to Martha in front of the mourners. For some reason, Edna simply hadn't obeyed him. She never understood where she had found the courage to cross him in such a sacred pact. At the funeral she had been quite self-possessed, except for the moment when she peered in the coffin and saw that without his icy blue eyes, Harry looked like a granite rock. His lifelong air of insistence was finally dulled as he lay there with his hands crossed over his silent heart.

Though she knew she owed it to Harry to give his message to Martha, something about his pushiness made her balk, something wasn't right. She had carried the obligation in her heart for a year but couldn't bring herself to deliver. She admitted to herself that Martha probably deserved to receive the apology, but the more time that passed, the less possible it seemed for Edna to say the words. They lived like a corpse in a bubble in her head, full of Harry's sour breath breathed out of his insistent, toothless mouth, hissed from the caverns of his skeletal cheeks: "Tell Martha I love her and I couldn't have wished for a better wife for my son."

Why should she embarrass herself now? There were no hard feelings anymore. Her daughter-in-law had doubtless sealed it all up long ago. Now Martha sent birthday cards, called Edna long-distance on the phone, even wrote her letters explaining modern-day psychology: *You should treat Will like a grown man. If you did, he could relate to you better and not be so distant.*

Edna peeked out the window again; they were coming up the walk now. She could see already that her son's shirt was hanging out in back. How could this be a grown man? *You have needs and they have to be met,* Martha had written. *You can only mourn so long, and then you need to get out in the world and turn your attention to other matters.*

With all due respect, what did the children know? Did they expect her to *date?* To make something of herself at this time of her life? She was lucky if she could drag herself into the kitchen for a cup of tea by noon every day. But at least Martha got on the phone once a week and talked to her like a regular human being, the opposite of what Will did. First of all, he'd get on after Martha was done talking and say, "Hello, Mother, this is your son Will." Who else could it be? Especially after he said "Hello, *Mother.*" Did she have any other sons? Did he think there was a brother born secretly out of wedlock whom he had to distinguish himself from? Then he said — and this infuriated Edna — "So how's everything?" Did he have even a pea-sized brain in that big head of his? Day after day she existed here alone, counting Harry's white hairs stuck to the rust-colored recliner; she looked out the window at the no-season California sky, going over and over how at the end of his life the doctors had turned her husband into a crazy drug addict. And Will asked her, *How's everything.*

What was taking them so long? She looked again. They had gone back to the car and were leaning into the trunk, picking out orange balls. Were they bringing her a game? Were they going to teach her how to juggle?

She couldn't tell, by any sense of expectation, if she had seen them weeks ago or years ago. They had come up north for the funeral, so it must have been just over a year ago. And they had come once before that, for Harry's last birthday party, when he was so sick.

Eileen, her youngest grandchild, looked tall and skinny. She was probably a throwback to someone on Martha's side; Martha came from a weak, skinny family. Edna's older granddaughters were chunky and solid, like her and Harry. Eileen was how old now — sixteen? almost seventeen? How did they grow up so fast? Wasn't it just yesterday she and Harry had been to Eileen's eighth-grade graduation in LA? And to the disastrous party afterward, where Will had been so rude? At the graduation and honors assembly the principal had called Eileen's name over and over—"Eileen Roth"—the same name as hers and Harry's! Eileen, embarrassed and smiling, went up and down the aisle like an usher at a movie theater, to claim first her silver pitcher, then her silver platter, then her silver urn. Her name was carved in each trophy for excellence in music, English, art. And then the certificates for academic honors, for community service, for heaven-knows-what else. Could this child be from her son with the heavy head? She doubted it. She had to give the credit to Martha. Will was like a rock. Dull and heavy. Not stupid, but not creative. He had driven her crazy banging on the piano when he was a teenager. A little grace she had hoped for, a little melody, a few show tunes. But no, he played Bach—that excuse for music! Not a sweet melody in twenty expensive music books. And then, worst of all, he played tunes from something called a *Passion,* singing along in Nazi German, gazing at record covers with Christ bleeding on the cross—and in a Jewish home, no less. For this they spent a fortune and gave Will piano lessons.

Then, as if all that weren't bad enough, he decided he was in love with Martha, the no-breast girl. Martha, compared to Edna, was a boy. Edna carried her breasts in a mammoth sling; the cloth of her brassieres was made of white canvas. Why should her son be stuck for life with a skinny girl like that? She and Harry asked him that a thousand times. But he was seventeen; his face was stubborn and ugly. They had said, "What do you need her for? She's not rich, she's not pretty. What do you have to make your mind up now for? You have years ahead of you to find someone better. The trouble with you is you're lazy. You settle on the first thing you see."

Bang on the piano! That's how he answered them. She wanted a boy like Al Jolson, and she got Will. She wanted a son who could play like Itzhak Perlman on the Ed Sullivan show so all the neighbors would envy her, and she got a banger on the keys.

The buzzer rang. She opened the door and stood back and let them pass by her like a hot wind. "Oranges from our tree, Grandma," Eileen said, holding out a handful of squashed, stunted oranges, pocked like golf balls. Edna looked at the child and was shocked. Didn't they own an iron at home? The girl was wearing a yellow blouse that looked worse than slept in. Worse than tied in a knot and jumped on. Nothing should look like that, not after two weeks in a tank, no less after a day's pleasant drive in a roomy car.

"You look good, Edna," said Martha, the daughter-in-law, leaning down to kiss her cheek. *A kiss she gives me, Harry,* she informed her husband, wherever he was. *Let's forget your message. We don't need to get sentimental now, with apologies, with tell-her-I-love-hers.* She felt a surge of irritation again at this duty assigned to her, this homework from the grave. Besides, Martha hadn't given her a *heartfelt* kiss, with a hug. It was cool, it was dutiful. The woman wasn't *that* wonderful. As for her son, he didn't even kiss her. He said, standing stiffly and as far from her as he could, "Hello, Mother, so how's everything?" He already looked blank. At least he didn't say, "This is your son Will."

When they filed in she realized the apartment needed painting. She had not had a healthy thought like that in this whole year while she was crying her eyes out. "You're wallowing in it, Mrs. Roth," the therapist at the senior citizen center had told her. "I have no sympathy for you at this point if you don't start pulling yourself together." Psychology—who needed it? Big words from big shots who didn't know what they were talking about. The first day, when she walked in crying two weeks after the funeral, a heartbroken woman, her life in crumbs, the therapist, with all her fancy degrees, said to her, spinning her pencil, "Come in, Mrs. Roth, and let me assure you of this— it's okay not to be okay." Sick to heart as she was, she didn't need permission from a thirty-year-old wearing eyeshadow and two earrings in each ear to cry her eyes out for her husband, a man who had died screaming like a maniac, "Get that nigger out of here!" If the doctors hadn't given Harry heroin, or whatever they gave him, he wouldn't have lost his mind and horrified that poor black minister in the other bed, whose eyes bulged like hard-boiled eggs when Harry screamed at him. Two weeks ago, because she was still crying like a faucet, Miss Earring Tree accused her of *wallowing.* What did that young woman know about grief? Or about listening all night to a voice on the radio talking about nuclear arms just so she didn't have to enter the vacuum of the dark, and see what she always saw, that picture in her mind, worse than Christ bleeding on the cross in those *Passion* records she had had to hide from Harry years ago so he didn't crack them on Will's head.

Will was on the couch now, looking around for something to read in the magazines on the coffee table. The magazines were two years old—they had been here during their last visit. Her son didn't like it here because there was nothing to read. If he wanted to read, let him go to a library.

She had thought she wanted them to come and visit her, but she could feel the problems starting already—this visit was just like all the other visits, years and years of visits. What she always forgot was that when Martha and Will walked in, she felt like brick walls had come sliding through the door to visit her. Years ago they used to come and leave the three girls for the night, in their green-flowered flannel sleeping bags, and the two of them would go off to a motel. A motel! What did they need to waste money for, she had a perfectly good hide-a-bed in the living room! In the morning they would come back sheepishly, the color slightly high in Will's large, sallow face, and refuse her breakfast of green-pepper pancakes, saying they had had coffee and doughnuts on the way over. The girls looked longingly at their mother's face as they sat there, picking squares of green pepper from their pancakes and lining them up around the edge of their plates.

But Harry had been there then, at least. Offering the children plates of candies, handfuls of nuts and raisins, coming at them like a waiter, every minute of the day, *Eat! Eat!* This annoyed her when he did it before dinner, but now she would give her eyes to have him spoil their appetites. She remembered how he had looked, holding high a dish of sugared gumdrops, his false teeth clattering at the children as he tempted them, even as she was rewarming the food she'd cooked in advance, the roast beef, the chicken, made the day before to give her plenty of time to clean up for the visit. She could see herself opening a can of bread (Boston baked brown bread), and Harry ruining their appetites with his gumdrops.

Eileen was looking restlessly out the window. What did the child think she was, a girl from India that she had to dress like that in a cheap Indian cotton blouse with loose threads all over it, with its yellow lacy sleeves, its tiny white buttons. Couldn't Martha shop

American for her daughter? Permanent press, at least? The trouble was there were right ways to do things, and they had never learned them.

"I see you got a new TV," Martha said. She was no longer skinny as a bean, but her breasts had not gotten anywhere in all these years.

"You know, I wonder if you could suffer from micro-valve proplapse," Edna said. "I saw a medical show last week and I was thinking of you — the doctor said women with small breasts who get depressed often have serious trouble with their micro-valves."

"Mitral," Will said from the couch.

"I'm not depressed," Martha said, "not in the slightest. Listen, Edna, what would you like to do while we're here? Go out for dinner in San Francisco? Take a ride up to see the redwoods?"

"I've been cooking for days," Edna said. "I have a roast turkey I made last week — I froze it, but I can defrost it with a little warming. I also have a big pot roast."

"Why do you cook so far in advance, Grandma?" Eileen asked. "Then it works out that you serve leftovers before you even serve a meal the first time."

"I *do* it this way," Edna said carefully, "because it works out very well. Then you have a variety of dishes to choose from. When you grow up, you'll realize there are ways to do things and ways not to do things." *For example,* Edna thought — it came to her like a vision. "For example," she said aloud, "the way your father behaved at the party after your eighth-grade graduation. That was a way *not* to do things."

Will glanced sideways out of his heavy-lidded eyes at Martha. Secrets and messages between them since they were seventeen. What kind of secrets could a son like Will have? He never told his mother anything. He only spoke up to her once, when he was seventeen. He had brought Martha to the house after school to play his records for her and he was taking her home and had no money. So Edna had doled out money to him, carfare money, and then he asked for money to buy something to eat. Edna had asked him in front of Martha — she had every right to know, she was *paying* — "Do you intend to pay for her? Do you need money for her, too?"

Later, when Will came home, too late, and she was waiting up for him ready with her speech about his seeing too much of Martha, he had fastened his turtle-eyes on her face and said, "Never talk like that in front of Martha again. Never call her *her* again." Edna would have liked to fight, her tongue was ready to go, but Will wouldn't stay to argue. He just clomped like a lead brick into his room and put on a record of something that sounded like cats braying and pots banging.

Now they were all here with nowhere to run to and she had something she had to get out of her system. Eileen could learn from this. They would have to stay and hear her out.

"Remember . . . you had a little party at your house after graduation from eighth grade," Edna said to Eileen. "Maybe you don't remember this. Some of your friends were there, and some of your parents' friends, and some of your teachers from high school."

"Just my English teacher," Eileen said.

"Yes, and when he left, when he announced to everyone that he was leaving" — Edna looked meaningfully at Will, who was now turning the pages of a two-year-old *Time* magazine — "do you remember what your father did? He sat there eating potato chips and waved good-bye. Do you know, Eileen, that you must *always* see your guests to the door? Your father just sat there, chewing, and he didn't budge an inch to show his guest to the door. That was unforgivable!"

Will threw down his magazine and looked at Martha.

"There are ways to do things, Will," Edna said loudly to her son. "It's a reflection on me when you don't do things right. And you should tuck in your shirt, right now," she added, for good measure.

"Edna . . . ," Martha began.

"I don't know how you've lived with him all these years. Here is a man who doesn't see his guests to the door."

"We don't have a very formal life, Edna. We don't have too many guests. . . ."

"No wonder!" She felt her mouth getting set, drawn down at the edges. Will had that same mouth.

"Look, Edna, we don't want to argue on this visit, so let me say something politely right at the start. You have to recognize that Will is grown up, and he's managed his life so far the way he wants to, and you just have to let him continue to manage it."

"He's not a millionaire, is he?" Edna demanded. "So don't tell me he's managed it so perfectly!"

"Well, he's doing all right. We have a nice life, nice kids — even you admit that — so why don't you just let him conduct his life the way he needs to, especially when he's in his own home. Maybe when he was little you wanted to teach him your ways, but now he's grown up. Look, he even has gray hair. He's all grown up." Martha smiled to make it seem less serious, but it was very serious.

Will suddenly stood up. "Let's go," he said to Martha. "Let's go home."

"You can't leave!" Edna said, feeling a stab of fear in her heart. "You can't leave me now. You're here to visit."

"We've visited long enough," Will said.

"I've prepared for this visit for days," Edna appealed to Martha. "I'm so alone here, so lonely without Harry."

Martha hardly looked vulnerable, hearing those words.

"Listen, Martha...Harry wanted me to tell you something very important. He gave me this message for you straight from the death-bed. He wanted me to tell you that he always loved you and there couldn't have been a better wife for his son."

Will mumbled something. "Oh sure...love...he really loved Martha, even when he practically threw her down the stairs."

Had Edna heard correctly? Had he really said that?

Eileen was standing in the kitchen, desperately twirling the handle on the can opener.

"He *loved* you, Martha," Edna insisted. She waited for Martha to dissolve with gratitude, but Martha had a slightly puckered look around her lips, as if she had just tasted one of those sour oranges from their own poisonous tree. Edna planned to throw them down the incinerator the instant she could.

"All these years, you and Dad...." Will had stopped mumbling and was speaking as if through a bullhorn. Edna threw him her stern-est, fiercest look, but the jolt didn't wither him.

"What *about* me and Dad?" she challenged him. Let him *dare* to say something cruel about his dead father. She saw Harry's face again, in that last pose, and she felt as if she might kill Will if he said one disrespectful word.

"Since you remember so perfectly, Mother, how I acted at a party at my own house, since you seem to want to discuss parties —," Will said, "remember that visit we had here just before Dad died? When all of us were up here for his last birthday party?" Her son's head hung on him like a grand piano. She couldn't believe she had given birth to this person.

"Do you really want Eileen to hear this?"

"Eileen remembers it," Will said. "Believe me, she remembers."

"Remembers what?"

"How you and Dad manipulated us! How you two ran the show and always have."

"What did we do?" She was truly worried; she didn't remember what they had done. She believed they had always acted the right way.

"Dad was already very sick. He had just come back from chemotherapy. He was in his maroon robe. And suddenly in the middle of dinner he jumped up and dialed his sister in Connecticut! We were all eating dinner, and he made this long-distance call!"

"So?"

"So he called his sister Rhoda and said 'Listen, Rhoda, the children and the grandchildren are here and they're all dying to talk to you!' Dying to talk to her? We were all eating dinner! My girls had never even met her, Martha had never met her. I barely remember her. *No one* wanted to talk to her. And Dad said, 'They're all standing in line here to talk to you,' and no one, not one of us, wanted to get up from the table, Remember, Eileen? *You* certainly didn't want to talk to Aunt Rhoda! You had nothing to say! Dad was taking advantage of his condition, he was manipulating all of us, embarrassing all of us because he was sick and dying."

At the word *dying* Edna began to cry.

"Your father loved you," she sobbed.

"That's not the *point*," Will said loudly.

"You have never been a sweet and loving son," Edna said to Will, recognizing that it was the awful, permanent truth.

"And you have got to stop running things!"

"Was it going to kill you to talk to his sister if it meant so much to him? if it would make him happy?"

"How happy did it make him? How happy did it make Aunt Rhoda?"

"He's dead," Edna said. "Your father is dead."

"That's right —," Will said, "so couldn't he have let us eat in peace the dinner you made in his honor? And then opened his presents cheerfully? Couldn't you *not* have made those wild faces at us to remind us that he was dying and was entitled to have his way this one last time? — entitled to keep on being a *tyrant!*"

"That's right, curse him now that he's dead and can't defend himself."

A tyrant! She had never let herself think the word. But hadn't he sent her running to the hospital candy machine to buy him a chocolate bar? Tubes in all his veins and no teeth, and he wanted a Hershey bar. His feet turning to ice already, and he was making plans to go to Miami Beach — he wanted her to order tickets right away. "Call the travel agent this minute!" he had ordered her, pointing at the phone beside his bed. His blue eyes were like comets headed for her brain. She jumped. "But first I want candy!"

She was in the hall, pulling the silver handle of the machine; it had taken her money but wouldn't give her the sweets, and the nurse had come running — *Hurry, hurry, this is it.* She got there too late. His head was thrown back, his mouth wide open, maybe to gulp in air or to give a scream, she would never know. But in her mind, day and night, was that picture of Harry, suffocating.

"Look," she said to Will, "this is how your father looked when he died." She threw her head back and opened her mouth as wide as it would go. She could feel her teeth expanding like the earth before an earthquake. She let her tongue fall forward. She rolled her eyes into her head. She held the pose for a full minute. Then she brought her head back down. "That's what I live with day and night," she said.

She looked at them, daring them to tell her to join organizations and make friends, to meet senior citizens, to keep her mouth shut while her granddaughter dressed like a ragamuffin and her son ate potato chips and let his guests wander to the door unattended.

Will had sunk back down on the couch. He picked up the magazine again. Edna wondered if she had imagined his speaking to her in that furious voice. Martha was standing at the wall, scrutinizing the wedding picture of her and Will displayed there. In it her face was completely hidden by Will's immense head.

Edna, moving with a light step, went into the kitchen and got down a handful of dinner plates. She handed them to Eileen to set around the table. Then from a hiding place inside the breadbox she took out a cut-glass candy dish full of gumdrops. They were huge and sticky — dense red, yellow, and green lumps glistening with sugar crystals. She began to pass them around to her guests. She held the dish under Will's nose. "Don't take too many," she said. "Not too many before dinner."

Tragic Lives

The beach was very wide and covered with soldiers resting on the sand, waiting to be let into the mess hall for breakfast. My mother was putting film into her camera and I was sitting on the low beach wall, peeling the layers of green skin from a baby coconut. I was five years old and wearing a new pinafore that was made in the shape of a blue and white butterfly. It was 1943 and we were in Miami Beach. My mother was going to take a picture of me to send back to my grandmother and my aunts in Brooklyn. My father was — as he had been for two weeks — out looking for a business to go into.

My mother, whose hair was long at the sides with bangs frizzed over the forehead, as was the style then, asked me to run out on the sand and pose for the picture. She held the camera to her eye. I pretended I was a butterfly flitting leisurely across the sand, and I hovered and dipped and lit here and there, until my mother, shading her eyes against the sun, finally called, "Stop right there." I stood on my toes and stretched my hands toward the sky, and my mother snapped the picture.

Thunderous applause came from every direction, and my mother and I stared with amazement at the hundreds of soldiers who had gathered around us and were clapping their hands together fiercely.

My mother, smiling a little, bent her head in embarrassment, and I ran to her and flung my arms around her, hiding my head in her skirt. Finally the terrible noise stopped, and when I looked out toward the beach I saw all the men moving away in a mass toward the mess hall, whose doors had just opened.

My mother, holding my hand tightly, walked with me down to the edge of the water, and in a few minutes we were the only ones left on the beach. For a while I squatted in the wet sand, dripping it through my fingers to make a lumpy design at my feet. Only the bottoms of my feet were white; the rest of me, since we had come here, had turned a deep brown color. My mother sat staring out to sea. Suddenly a gray shadow blew over us, and in a few minutes heavy drops were hitting us on the head. The sudden rains came nearly every day, and it was always great fun as we laughed and rushed for cover, getting wet, but not minding it because the air was so hot.

This time my mother took my hand and we ran across the beach toward Ocean Avenue. The closest building was the mess hall, and we stood against its outer wall, but there was no overhang and the rain came down more and more heavily. I began to shiver, and my mother, seeing no alternative, moved with me to the open door. Inside we could see the rows of tables and all the soldiers sitting at them, eating.

We stood stiffly just inside the doorway, facing out toward the beach, and after a moment or two a soldier came over and knelt down in front of me. He was very handsome; he had a dimple in one cheek and a warm smile.

"Would you like a Hershey bar?" he said to me, pulling one from his pocket. I looked at my mother and she nodded and I took it shyly, staring down at his big shoes.

He stood up to his full height and said to my mother, "I'm getting in practice for what I'll be doing over there."

"Do you know for sure that you're going?" my mother said.

"We're shipping out in two days," he said. Then he touched me on the head and said, "Is your daddy over there, too, honey?"

"He isn't in the army," I said.

My mother said nothing, and for a few seconds the soldier stood there, looking at me with something in his eyes that reminded me of when my uncles tossed me in the air and nuzzled my neck and said I was adorable.

Finally the soldier said, "Actually, no one's really allowed in here but military personnel. . .they're pretty strict about that."

"Well, the rain's stopping," my mother said. "Thank you for the candy."

"My pleasure," the soldier said, and my mother smiled at him. Outside, as she held my hand tightly and hurried with me back to the hotel, she said, with something like reverence in her voice, "Some of those men are going to have tragic lives."

My mother's family was notorious for tragic lives. Her only brother, Saul, at the age of nineteen, rented a fishing boat with a friend on a stormy Yom Kippur day and the two were never seen again. For years after that, my mother's older sister, Rachel (older by twelve years), and my grandmother were called to the city morgue to identify the remains of drowned men, in case any of them might be my lost uncle. None of them ever were. My grandmother took to visiting mediums, begging them to contact her son. Up to then a very sensible, practical, peasantlike woman, she became a student of seances and a frequenter of fortune tellers. My mother's delicate younger sister, who had her own emotional problems, was driven half-mad by the ordeal and became a recluse.

A few years later, while my mother was still in her teens, her father developed a disease known as Ludwig's Angina, which resulted in the floor of his mouth swelling so severely that he began to suffocate. When a neighborhood doctor was called in the middle of the night and told that my grandfather was in great distress, he complained that it was late, and that it only sounded like a sore throat. He would come to see my grandfather the next morning. An hour after that, my grandfather was carried down the stairs on a stretcher to an ambulance. As he passed by my mother, who was waiting on the steps, he said to her with what breath he had left, "Button your coat so you don't catch cold." He died on the way to the hospital.

My mother told me these tales over the years, as soon as she thought I was old enough to absorb them. She watched my face as she told me the stories, as if to correct me if I didn't show the appropriate awe and respect for them. Their importance went without question.

Of less immediate importance (but important enough) was the story of a second cousin of ours who lived in the Bronx, a girl who had been dropped on her head as a baby and had always been a little slow as a result, who married in her thirties an Italian man who, it was said, treated her roughly. He refused to allow her to attend any of the family functions at which he was required to appear, and one Easter Sunday, when her husband went alone to the wedding of one of the relatives in his extended family, she turned on the gas jets in her kitchen and killed herself. I was given the news that same Easter Sunday as I was playing stoopball in front of our house in Brooklyn. Dozens of Christian families were passing by on their way to church, the little girls wearing dresses made of tiers of organdy, and white straw hats with ribbon streamers down the back. Church bells were tolling, and my aunt and my mother stood on the steps above me, tears on their cheeks, telling me about the death of this poor woman. For years after that, I thought that death must be the sound of church bells tolling.

We lived in the Belle Vista, a run-down old apartment hotel on the ocean, one of the few buildings that wasn't completely occupied by troops. In the evenings after I was tucked in bed, my mother and father would go outside to sit in the tiny courtyard, leaving me alone in the apartment, with a dim yellow light bulb burning in the hall. I could hear their voices through the open window as they talked to the manager of the hotel. They talked only of the war. That was all anyone ever talked about.

One night I followed my father when he took out the garbage after dinner, and as we stepped into the dark back alley, a soldier shouted, "Halt! Who goes there?" He shoved a rifle at us, pointing it at my father's stomach.

"A civilian," my father said, "taking out the garbage."

The soldier, wearing an MP band around his arm, looked at my father contemptuously. "You here on vacation?"

"No, I have a business here."

"Your business is over there," the soldier said.

"I'm too old," my father answered apologetically. "I have a wife and a child."

"You don't look too old to heft a rifle. It doesn't take much muscle. Here, want to see if you can lift this one? It isn't any heavier than that garbage."

Later that evening I was pretending to fish in the bathtub. I often watched the old people fishing on the pier. I had attached a wafer cracker to a string, and had put a green segmented toy snake in the tub, to act as my fish. I sat on the rim and watched the water turn green as the paint from the snake drifted out in wavery lines. From the other room I heard my father say, "I keep thinking I ought to join up."

My mother said, "We have someone in already. My sister Rachel's son Jerry is enough. One badly wounded from our family is enough."

"Jerry isn't me," my father said. "I'm not doing my part."

"I don't want to have a telegram delivered to me one of these days," my mother said. "You're helping out by making the recordings. They're all some of the boys' families are going to have left of them. You're doing your part by running the business."

"I feel sometimes as if I have to join up."

"You have a wife and a child," my mother said. "No one expects you to. And besides, I'm almost certain now we're having another."

"What makes you certain?"

"I vomit every morning," my mother said. "I turn my insides out."

The business my father had opened was a little recording studio on Washington Avenue next door to a photography shop that had a big sign in front of it which my mother read to me: SEND YOUR *SMILE* HOME TO YOUR MOM, YOUR BEST GIRL, YOUR WIFE. The little store was furnished with a backdrop of palm trees, heavy with coconuts, and a place for a soldier to stand just in front of it while his picture was being taken.

My father, after checking with the owner of the shop, put up a sign on his shop that said: SEND YOUR *VOICE* HOME TO YOUR MOM, YOUR BEST GIRL, YOUR WIFE.

There was a little booth in the store, enclosed all around by a heavy brown curtain. When a soldier came in, my father would seat him in the booth, give him a microphone to hold, and then, as he pulled the curtain closed, would give the go signal. The recording machine was outside the booth, a heavy metal machine that stood on the floor, spinning out black flax as the needle cut the record. My father always went to stand outside the store while the soldier talked, holding his stop watch to check the time remaining on the record. I often stayed next to the machine, collecting the springy strands of warm black plastic as they came off the record, and listening to the soldier speak into the microphone:

Dearest Caroline Honey,
Here I am in Miami Beach where it's the middle of winter and I'm sweating like the devil. If you were here with me we could really have another great honeymoon. I don't know yet when we're going over, but it will be pretty soon. Don't worry about me. Before you know it we'll finish this war up the way it should be finished, and I'll be home and we'll be together again. . . .
We're camped out in a big hotel. I'm not lucky enough to have a room, so I sleep in the cocktail lounge with a hundred other guys. One of these days, maybe you and me can settle down here in Florida, which is a Paradise on Earth. It's always summer and when it rains, it only rains on one side of the street. Keep your chin up, kiddo, and keep that Victory Garden growing.

Occasionally, after my father had started the record going, the soldier in the booth could think of nothing to say, and under the brown curtain I could see his feet scuffing and tapping nervously on the floor. My mother had written a few sample letters — to Mothers, to Wives, and to Best Girls — for my father to offer as suggestions, but my father seemed embarrassed to proffer them to the tongue-tied soldiers. One day a soldier came in, singing like Frank Sinatra, but when he got in the booth he was paralyzed. "Say, would you please shut off the record and wait till I can think of something to say?" he called out desperately from the booth. My father said, "Relax. Just sing a song. She'll love it." And the soldier did.

I spent a lot of time in the hotel with my mother, listening to "Let's Pretend" and the "White Rabbit Bus" when they were on the radio.

My mother spent hours retching in the bathroom, and when it was time to eat, she could only eat slices of chilled tomato, sprinkled with salt.

At six each morning, we were awakened by the soldiers marching in the streets — "Hup, two, three, four." Out my window I watched them — the legs of the men opening and closing like so many hinges. Sometimes they sang as they marched: "Off we go, into the wild blue yonder, flying high, into the sun. . . . " My mother looked at the soldiers, and then at my father still sleeping on the studio couch, and it seemed to me her lips curled in contempt.

When he was awake, she could not — because of her fear — do enough for him. She saw to it that he was fed, comfortable, and distracted. She didn't want him to think about the war because if he thought about it enough, he would leave her. And she would be left a widow and I a fatherless child. And yet I knew that she, like me, wished he were one of those marvelous, brave soldiers.

Soon there began to be blackouts at night. There were sirens, and then we had to sit in the dark, waiting for it to end. I said I was afraid of the war, and my father said it was all right, that the enemy was far away, across the ocean. After that I was afraid of the ocean.

My father often took me walking on the pier, and I watched the pelicans grabbing up fish, taking them right along with the fishermen's lines, hooks, and sinkers, the sacks under their jaws growing heavier and more taut until I thought they would burst. One old man reeled in his line, and as his fish flapped up from the water, a pelican swallowed it. He was furious, and he kept reeling in the line till the pelican came flopping onto the pier. Then the old man sat down on the bird while he pried open the creature's beak to get out his rightfully caught fish. The pelican had a mass of dead fish, uneaten, flattened in his pouch.

Then everyone forgot the bird because a troop ship came steaming past the pier toward the dock. It was listing to the side, as the men all crowded to the rail to wave and shout at all of the people on the pier. The soldiers, all clumped together in their brown uniforms like so many Tootsie Rolls, were shouting and leaping up and down. My father clasped the wooden railing of the pier until his knuckles went white. He stared at the ship. Then his pipe, which he was holding loosely in his mouth, slipped from between his lips and fell into the water with a dull splash.

He raised both hands and began to wave wildly.

"Jerry! Jerry!"

My father nearly fell into the ocean. Then he jerked me along after him, pulling me so fast I was flying. When the ship docked, we were there to grab my cousin Jerry, to hug him and to smack him on the back. He held me high in the air, and I grabbed for the shiny brim of his lieutenant's hat. There were golden wings pinned to it. He had a dimple in one cheek, just like the soldier in the mess hall, but his smile was more beautiful because of the love in it. His khaki shirt was stiff and creased in perfectly straight box-shape lines. He had little gold wings pinned on both points of his shirt collar. His belt buckle shone in the sunlight.

He carried me on his shoulders for as long as we stayed with him, and he promised to come over to the hotel as soon as he could get away. We rushed back to my mother to tell her what had happened. The surprise of our meeting Jerry — a wild stroke of luck — made the three of us happy for the whole day.

He came to see us for dinner the next evening, and said his unit was being transferred to the Pacific the morning after. My mother broiled lamb chops for him, and when he had trouble manipulating his knife my mother asked him what was wrong.

"Just a little pain," he said. "The old shrapnel wound. Nothing much. They got most of it out. Next time I'll duck. If you know how, it's like walking between raindrops."

My father was quiet all evening, but my mother kept asking questions about places, about battles, about the danger; Jerry said he couldn't answer her. "When this war is over, I'll tell you everything. I keep telling Mom and Hildy that, too. When I can, I'll tell everyone everything. The news on the radio is usually two or three days behind us. And it's usually wrong."

"Your mother is very worried," my mother said to him.

"I'm not interested in hearing that!" he said angrily. "Look, don't you people know we have to get this thing settled, and settled the right way? I don't want to come home, and be sitting around the dinner table, and they'll call me up again after another surprise like we had on December 7th to tell me to come back and finish it off. We have to finish it off right now!"

My father stood up and walked once around the room and then out the door.

Jerry finished his lamb chops and came over to me.

"I got you a beautiful little doll in England. It's still in my trunk because I didn't know I'd be bumping into you, but I'll mail it to you as soon as I can. It has blue eyes like you have, and pink cheeks like you have, and long beautiful eyelashes."

"I wish I could have some wings," I said.

Soon my father came back, and he was carrying a carton of ice cream. We all had some for dessert. When Jerry had to leave, my father shook his hand very hard, and for a very long time.

"Take it easy, kid. Good luck over there."

"I'm always careful," Jerry said.

My mother phoned her sister Rachel to tell her about Jerry's visit. She said she was sorry she had forgotten to have him make a recording of his voice for her and for Hildy — it just hadn't crossed her mind.

The day after Jerry left, my mother took me with her to the Red Cross Meeting Hall, where she and other women rolled bandages for the wounded soldiers. I was allowed to unroll the gauze across the table as the women cut it to size. We went there to roll bandages every afternoon that my mother felt well enough to go.

A few weeks later I got the English doll Jerry had bought me. I named her Alice. She had blue eyes and black painted curls and an embroidered blue dress. Jerry had pinned a tiny pair of gold wings to the dress. The first minute I played with the doll I dropped her and her china head cracked in two. My mother said not to worry, that dolls for children should never be made out of china in the first place.

When we got a V-mail letter from Jerry, my mother read it to us:

I still think about those lamb chops. Can't say where I am now, but we're seeing action. It's really hot as hell here. Took off the top of some trees the other day. Never saw them going up the ridge. Put a dent in my right engine. Got a terrible razzing from the boys. Called me "the old woodcutter." Plane was the only one hurt. First time I nicked one of Uncle Sam's

*aircraft. Makes me mad. Must be getting careless. Don't
worry — gonna fly higher from now on.*

My mother listened to the news all the time. She told me angrily to
be quiet if I spoke while the radio was on. Soon she could not eat anything — even cold tomatoes made her throw up. One morning she
said to my father, "I have a feeling . . . go down and buy the newspaper."

"What kind of feeling?"

"Go. Buy the paper."

My father listened to her. When he came back he didn't want to
hand her the paper. She ripped it from him. The War Department
listed Jerry as "missing in action." My mother kept rubbing her
thighs and crying, "I can't feel my legs. They've gone dead."

My father said, "I'm going to join up."

"Do you want to kill me?" my mother begged.

"We're both half dead as it is," he answered.

Jerry's picture was printed in the New York *Sun,* and with it the letter to Jerry's mother from his closest buddy, Lt. Robert Allen of Pat-
erson, New Jersey:

Dear Mrs. Hornstein:

*I was in the flight over the forests of New Guinea that
day with Jerry. In fact, my ship was just behind his when the
bombs were dropped from above us. Luckily, I was at the
closest point to home, for which I headed. I last saw Jerry's
ship follow the others in flight. When we met at the coast,
one ship was missing. That was Jerry's. There isn't much else
to say except that all hope should not be given up. I want you
to keep hoping and praying, just as I am.*

Letters seemed the most important things in those days, except for
telegrams. Everyone was waiting for mail. A letter soon came ad-
dressed to my father from his draft board in Brooklyn. Because of
the emergency war situation it had become necessary for the government to draft older men and men with families. My father would be
drafted unless he was employed within three weeks in an authorized
defense job.

"All right, then," my mother said, "we'll go home, and you'll get a
job in a defense plant."

"We'll see about what I'll do when we get home," my father said, "but yes, we'll definitely go home. Maybe if I can get you and the little one settled in with your family, then I can join up."

"You might as well put a gun to your head," my mother said.

Because my mother was having a difficult pregnancy, her doctor told her a train trip would not be a wise choice. He got special permission for her to fly to New York on a troop carrier, but there was only space for her — my father and I would have to take the train back. My mother said she refused to spend the trip gagging into a paper bag in front of a thousand soldiers, and she would take the train with us. My father said he could not fight with her about everything. We left the Miami train station in a temperature of close to 100°, and when we got to New York it was snowing.

The first night back we slept at my Aunt Rachel's house, and in the middle of the night my mother began to hemorrhage. In the morning she miscarried the baby that would have been my brother.

My father took a job in an airplane factory, manufacturing wings for bombers, and after two weeks he destroyed a wing because he didn't know how to work the machinery properly. When the metal wing snapped, a piece of it tore open an artery in my father's arm, but still they accused him of being a saboteur and he was put under surveillance.

We learned of many search parties combing through the jungles of New Guinea, but Jerry was not among the men discovered, or among those who just "walked out of the forest." Even so, the War Department kept his status listed as "missing in action," and did not change it to "killed in action."

My Aunt Rachel received a letter from the Army Effects Bureau stating that the footlocker and its contents belonging to Lt. Jerry Hornstein were being forwarded to her and that such action "does not of itself vest title in you. The property is transmitted in order that you may safely keep it on behalf of the owner, pending change in his status."

It seemed to everyone that it was still possible to hope.

When my Aunt Rachel received the trunk, she found in it Jerry's diary, but the pages that must have been written in the days just before his disappearance had been ripped out. The Army Effects Bureau wrote again: "It is regretted that this Bureau has no information regarding the pages which you say were removed from the diary belonging to your son. You may be assured that in the event additional belongings of Lt. Hornstein's are received here, prompt disposition will be made."

In the fall I began to go to school, and my father continued to work in the airplane factory. One day, while watching my mother clean a chicken, I swung on a towel rack, which broke off the edge of the sink. I fell and broke my arm. I screamed when the doctor twisted the bone into place, but I was proud of my cast, because now I was suffering, too.

Yet the suffering was less terrible all around us. When the telegram boy came up the block on his bicycle, we no longer watched with terror in our hearts to see where he would stop. He had already come to our house. Then, finally, when we had stopped wishing for it, the war ended. It was over.

My mother saw an article in the New York *News,* titled "Lindy Over Shangri-La." According to the article, Charles Lindbergh had flown low over an isolated spot in the New Guinea jungle and discovered a primitive valley in Dutch New Guinea. There he saw three C-47 transports, an A-20 attack bomber, a Douglas dive bomber, and two British planes which had made emergency landings and had been stranded because they could not take off in the rarefied air on a short runway. My mother wrote and asked the newspaper how she could get in touch with Mr. Lindbergh, and she was told that he could be contacted care of the Ford Motor Company, Detroit, Michigan.

Mr. Lindbergh answered her inquiry with this letter:

> *I am extremely sorry to have to tell you, in reply to your letter, that the newspaper report about my seeing an isolated place in New Guinea, cut off from communications, where several planes had made forced landings, is untrue, as are so many similar stories printed these days.*
> *I want you to know that you have my deepest sympathy in your great concern for your nephew who has been reported*

*missing. I wish I had information which might be of value
to you.*

> *Sincerely,*
> *Charles A. Lindbergh*
> *The Tompkins House*
> *Long Lots Road*
> *Westport, Conn.*

Jerry's dear buddy, Lt. Robert Allen, often came to visit my Aunt
Rachel and to talk to her about Jerry. Jerry's girlfriend, Hildy, also
came to talk to Aunt Rachel and to grieve with her. Soon Lt. Robert
Allen and Hildy became close friends. One day they married each
other.

Eventually my father and mother and I moved into a little house
that had a lilac tree in front of it and in the backyard, for me, a swing
hanging from a mulberry tree. My father went into a new business.
My mother longed for and mourned for the son who would have
been named Jerry if he had lived, and she was not kind to my father
for a long time. He was not like her. He did not understand her. He
was unscathed. But she had become one of those who had a tragic
life.

Someone Should Know This Story

I had no interest at all in spending the weekend with Carolyn, especially on such short notice, and also because Carolyn communicated most of her ideas to me by pushing, shoving, and jolting me about.

She was not really a friend of mine, but a girl of fourteen, my own age, who happened to be the daughter of my Aunt Ava, who was not really an aunt of mine, but the wife of a man who once asked my mother to marry him when he was just out of law school and she was a legal secretary in a firm where he applied for a job.

I could tell my mother wanted me to accept Ava's spur-of-the-moment invitation — it had something to do with being very civilized about her relationship with Ava, and it seemed important to Ava, too, that I "dump my nightie and a toothbrush in a bag and come right along."

Ava had driven into Brooklyn to visit her old mother who was in a rest home on Ocean Parkway, and she had dropped in to see us "for old times sake." When she arrived, my mother had just come up from the basement with a heavy wicker basket full of wet laundry. By the time I had led Ava and Carolyn through the length of the house to the back porch, my mother was already leaning out over the railing, pushing the clothesline across the yard. They talked over the squeaking of the pulley.

Although I rarely liked to help with the wash (it was only in the winter I enjoyed being there when it was pulled in, every shirt and pajama frozen stiff by the cold), I stood beside my mother and shook out towels, getting them ready to hand to her with two clothespins for hanging.

"We send our clothes out to the laundry," Carolyn said, poking me fiercely in the ribs and laughing. She had buck teeth, but even so she was attractive because she had large breasts and a small waist like her mother, and brilliant straight dark black hair. Ava wore her black hair pulled back in a perfect chignon, with a string of colored stones woven somehow through the bun.

My mother's short wavy hair was nearly white—even though she was only in her early forties, she was often taken by my schoolfriends to be my grandmother—and I experienced a queer loyalty toward her just then, as she stood pushing the clothesline across the yard, wearing flat straw shoes and a seersucker housedress.

Ava wore high-heeled pumps and carried a shoulder bag made out of a whole alligator—I could count the teeth in the alligator's mouth as she stood talking to my mother.

"Herbert would be so pleased to have Janet stay with us. He's so fond of her."

I liked Herbert very much myself, but it was a feeling I never mentioned. Years before, he had come to our house on the pretext of some legal service he was doing for my grandmother, and he had seen me standing in the doorway beside my mother. As if I were not present, he said to her, sadly, "You know, Anna, she could have been mine."

"Why don't you go, Janet?" my mother asked me. "It will be a nice change."

I thought about my plans for the weekend: on Saturday I was going to take my grandmother to the movies, where we would get another flowered china cup to add to our growing set of dishes, and on Sunday several of my friends were going to come over to play canasta on the back porch. I looked about the backyard, where my dog was sleeping in his doghouse, where the lilacs were just starting to bud on the tree, where my little sister was sitting on the grass, coloring in her coloring book, and I thought of spending a weekend being shoved about by Carolyn.

"I can't go," I said. "My piano recital is June 10th, and I have to practice."

"Nonsense," Ava said. "We have the Steinway and no one ever touches it. Carolyn took lessons for six weeks and that was the end of that. We'll close you in the living room whenever you want to practice and you'll have perfect privacy."

If my father had been home he would have helped me out of it. He had no use for this occasional but continuing friendship with Herbert and Ava, and took no part in it. He considered Herbert to be a weak, scrawny asthmatic, and as far as reckoning with the visibly great material rewards Herbert lavished on his family as a result of his education, ambition, and successful legal practice—well, my mother had always been a free agent, and could have married anyone she chose. My father, who dealt in antiques, was not about to bow his head in shame.

I packed my clothes, and the blue sheet-music edition of "Claire de Lune," and drove back to Manhattan with Carolyn and Ava, my eyes tearing all the while from the smoke of Ava's cigarette filling the interior of the black Buick.

I was introduced first to the doorman and then to the elevator man. Several women with packages were coming into the building just then, and we were packed against the walls of the elevator with hardly room to breathe. No one said hello to Ava, and she stared ahead haughtily, taller than anyone in the car.

As soon as we got into the carpeted hallway of the sixth floor, I noticed the absence of air. It was springtime and there was no air on Park Avenue. No backyard, no grass, no flowers, no pets. How did they live here?

But in a moment I saw there were cut flowers in a silver vase on the dining room table, and I was shown the house pet from a distance: "His name is Malachi, and he will not hurt you unless he is provoked." Ava smiled briefly at me, and went down the hall into her bedroom.

"What provokes him?" I asked Carolyn. The dog was a huge, unattractive collie; he lay under the piano, staring at us and breathing heavily.

"Just don't go near him," Carolyn said, punching my shoulder for emphasis. "Come on, follow me."

In the kitchen I met Suellen, a black woman who scowled at

Carolyn and said, "Don't you ask me what's for dinner. Whatever it is, it'll have to suit you."

"What's that?" I asked, pointing at a machine screwed into the wall.

"An ice crusher," Carolyn said. "Don't you have one?"

"No, we don't." I felt suddenly very frightened and trapped. There was nothing here I wanted to do, no one I wanted to be with or even liked. Herbert was kind, but I knew he would have very little to do with me.

I considered for a moment phoning my father at his store, and begging him to come and get me. I knew he would—he would come in an instant. But just the thought of him calmed me; the way he loved me was so tremendous that I could survive anything as long as I remembered him. My mother sometimes said she thought she had been destined for some other life, with a man of breeding, education, money. Of all her boyfriends, most of whom had been young lawyers, only my father was working in the pajama department of Loeser's when she met him. It never occurred to me to ask her why she actually married him, a man with an eighth-grade education, since it seemed obvious to me he would have been the best possible choice in the world—for anyone.

And yet, sometimes I saw her watching him work with his huge powerful hands, with dirt that was as permanent as his skin embedded under his nails, watching him move some heavy oak chifforobe he had just bought, his face red with the strain of the labor (once he cracked two ribs and did not know it for days), or watching him peer through a loupe at pieces of old jewelry he kept in a cigar box—and I saw on her face a certain distance, maybe distaste or self-pity, maybe regret that she had come to spend her days with a man who had never read Shakespeare's sonnets. I knew that in our bookcase we had the sonnets, given to my mother by Herbert, and inscribed by him to her. If my father had seen it there, or minded it, I never knew.

Ava came out of her bedroom, dressed in a long silk robe, and went down the hall into another room. Even though this was an apartment, it seemed to have more rooms than our whole house did. There were antiques on all the polished surfaces of the furniture, and

I could tell they existed here in a different sense than did the ones in my father's store. Here they were works of art, carefully dusted and displayed, while in my father's shop antiques were piece goods, merchandise, to be traded and sold, with profit the only goal in mind. In our own home we had no antiques. My mother could not stand them. To her they were just "old things" that belonged to "other people."

Carolyn threw her arms around me and bear-hugged me from behind. I gasped, and stood trying to catch my breath. "I just can't believe you're here," she said. She dragged me by the hand to where her mother was in a little alcove, talking on the phone. "Get bonbons," she whispered, and her mother made an impatient gesture with her hand for Carolyn to be quiet. Ava was ordering cuts of beef, fruit, vegetables, rolls and pastries.

"If your mother shops on the phone," I asked Carolyn in a whisper, "how can she be certain they won't send her rotten tomatoes and bad meat?"

"Simple," Carolyn said, so sure of herself. "We'd never call that grocer again."

I thought of the way my mother shopped, pushing our old black-wicker baby stroller to the Avenue, stopping at each store to stand in line—the fish market, the bakery, the drugstore, the delicatessen. And what exactly were bonbons?

When Herbert came home he was carrying a sheaf of papers. He saw me sitting on the couch and smiled gently at me. "Is your mother here?" he asked softly, eyebrows raised.

"No. Aunt Ava was in Brooklyn today, and she brought me back to spend the night."

"Oh, Brooklyn, yes," Herbert said. He wheezed badly. He wore glasses and was going bald.

"Ava?" he called. He looked at Carolyn. "She's not in with Ravi, is she?"

"Of course not," Carolyn said. Something hard passed between them. "She's steaming her face." When her father had gone down the hall to his room, Carolyn mumbled, "She's not a fool, you know."

When we were all seated around the dinner table, Ava rang a silver bell and the maid came in with the first course. Dinner took a very long time, and there was no conversation. After each course was finished, Ava rang the bell and the maid appeared. Everyone seemed quite miserable, waiting and waiting while each place was cleared and the next dish brought. Finally Herbert cleared his throat and said, "Well, Janet, how do you like it in this neck of the woods?"

"It's fine, Uncle Herbert," I said. "It's very interesting."

After dessert I asked Carolyn which room was the bathroom. She pointed down the hall, and when I opened the door I thought she meant, I saw a dark young man sitting at a desk, wearing a turban on his head.

He stood up slowly. "How do you do?" he said with great significance. His teeth were brilliantly white in his dark face, and I experienced a kind of thrill that I had never felt before. He was evaluating me as if I were a grown woman.

"Excuse me," I said. "I didn't mean to open your door. I didn't know anyone else lived here."

"They try to keep it a secret," he said, with some soft laughter. "It would be embarrassing for anyone to know they were down on their luck and had to take in a boarder."

I knew I could not stand in the doorway and engage in conversation. "Pardon me," I said again, "I'm sorry," and I backed out quickly and closed the door. I was breathless when I came back into the dining room; I was reminded of the days, not so long ago, when I used to read Nancy Drew mystery stories, in which just such discoveries were commonplace.

"Why don't you two girls do something?" Ava suggested. "What do you do with your friends at home, Janet?"

"We like to play canasta," I said.

Ava said, "Carolyn has a nice puppet collection in her room. Why don't you both go in there and play for a while?"

In the morning when I awoke, Carolyn was not in her bed. I put on my skirt and blouse and went down the hall to the kitchen. Suellen said to me, "She has a riding lesson every Sunday morning. She said she forgot to tell you, but she'll be back by noon. The riding school comes and gets her at 8:30, and she didn't want to wake you. She said you should wait for her and practice the piano."

"Where is my aunt?"

"Asleep. But she's got a lady coming here in a little while, and we got to clear the kitchen. What do you like to eat? There's some French toast left."

She served it to me covered with maple syrup; at home my mother sprinkled a little sugar and cinnamon on it, and that was the way I liked it. I had never realized that life for other people could be so different in so many ways.

As I passed down the hall I could hear Herbert wheezing in his room. I heard the whoosh-whoosh of his rubber atomizer. I got "Claire de Lune" from my suitcase and went into the living room, where the dog was lying under the piano. He growled softly as I pulled out the bench. I hoped that French piano music would not provoke him.

I practiced for at least an hour, for the first time really happy to have a reason to work out the hardest passages. I simply could think of nothing as acceptable to pass the time as playing my music. I hoped that at least one good result of this visit would be that I might do nicely at my recital.

I wondered when they were going to take me home. Since no one talked very much here, I felt it would be impolite to ask anything outright. I had had trouble sleeping, and my stomach hurt during the night. I considered trying to find the bathroom in the dark, but I wasn't absolutely sure which room belonged to the dark young man, and I couldn't take a chance. Just before we went to bed, I had asked Carolyn about him.

"Oh, Ravi," she said. "He's an Indian prince or something. He's a student at the university and he lives with us because we have so much extra room. My father hates him, but my mother likes him."

"Do you like him?"

"It doesn't matter," she answered. "He has no use for me."

When I was through practicing I went into the kitchen for a glass of water. Ava was lying naked on a towel on the kitchen table, and a woman was slapping her back with both hands. I stood in the doorway watching. The woman, who was dressed in a white uniform just like Suellen, hit Ava's back with the sides of her hands, and then the flat of them. The smacks were hard enough for me to hear. There were bottles of lotions and powders on the counter. Ava's head, wrapped in a towel, rested on her arms. Her eyes were closed.

I went quickly down the hall past Herbert's bedroom, where he was wheezing more loudly than before. I didn't know where to go — in the living room was the unfriendly dog, the maid had disappeared, and at the end of the hall was the Indian prince. There was no outside to go to, and Carolyn had no books of the kind I liked to read. Her parents seemed to buy her only games and books that were suitable for an eight-year-old.

The door at the end of the hall opened suddenly and the prince came out. "Good morning," he said, bowing. "May I ask if you are a cousin of the family's?"

"I'm not related," I said. "My mother once almost married Carolyn's father, but I don't think that makes me anything here."

"What a shame," he said.

"That I'm not related?"

"That Herbert didn't marry your mother. No doubt he could have been a much happier man."

"How do you know?" I asked.

"I live here, my dear," he said, smiling. We stood very close together in the hall. He must have been on his way out, for he was holding a briefcase in his hand.

"That is a strange noise," he said. We could hear the slaps resounding down the hall.

"My aunt has some woman . . . working on her in the kitchen."

"On Sunday?" the prince said. "How unusual." He set his briefcase down on the floor. "I won't go out after all," he said.

He remained there, looking at me and smiling. My heart pounded. I thought of the puppets, which suddenly seemed something attractive I wanted to play with.

"You have extraordinary blue eyes," the prince said. "You also play the piano with dedication. One day you will be an interesting and beautiful woman."

"Excuse me," I said. I turned around and rushed to Herbert's door. I knocked on it.

"Come in," he said. He was in an armchair by the window, reading the newspaper. On the table beside him were his atomizer, his medicine, and a cup of coffee.

"Do you think you could take me home early, Uncle Herbert?" I asked him. "I'm really not feeling very well."

"I think Ava was planning to take you home this afternoon," he said.

"But couldn't you? Now?"

"Let me tell you the truth about this, Janet. Ava doesn't like me to see your mother very much. You know, in the old days I was very fond of your mother, and Ava is still jealous."

I wondered if I should tell him that I thought my father was also jealous of him.

Herbert said, "I wonder — do you know that I once asked your mother to marry me?"

"Yes, of course I know that."

"Do you know the circumstances? Did she ever tell you about it? How we went to a Chinese restaurant that night?"

I shook my head.

"Someone should know this story," he said.

I sat down.

"We'd been going out for a long time. Your mother was not a passionate person, it was never easy to know her feelings. We went to plays and concerts and she seemed to enjoy my company. Your grandmother liked me a great deal — in fact, I think she even began to love me like a son — and I was very optimistic. I bought your mother a diamond engagement ring. We went to dinner that night, and when she reached for a fortune cookie, I stopped her hand and said, 'Here, your future is in this little box.' She looked at the ring and she refused it. I insisted she take it, that it was for her and that I didn't want it back even if she didn't accept my proposal. She handed it to me, and I handed it back to her, and finally she just dropped it on the table. When we got up to leave, we each thought the other would feel he must go back and get it, but neither of us did. We left it on the white tablecloth."

"Forever?" I asked.

"Forever."

"My mother has no diamond rings now," I told Herbert.

He finished his coffee and then said he would check with Ava about taking me home. I followed him down the hall. Ava was no longer lying naked on the kitchen table. The woman in white was packing up her bottles of lotions and powders. The sound of Ava's laughter came from the prince's room.

"Come! Come!" Herbert said suddenly. "*I'll* take you home. Quickly . . . get your things."

I didn't wait to say good-bye to Carolyn, nor did I ever thank Ava. Herbert drove me all the way back to Brooklyn without speaking to me. He wasn't angry or distant, he was just thoughtful, and I began to relax and let my guard down. I put my head back against the seat and almost fell asleep.

When we pulled up to my house, no one was in the front garden, but my dog was asleep under the beach chair and my father's pipe rested on its wooden arm. Just then my mother came to the front door to shake out the dry mop, and she saw us. She smiled and waved. Her white hair shone in the sun.

Herbert and I got out of the car, and he carried my small suitcase to the bottom of the front stoop. He looked up at my mother, who stood on the top step.

"Daddy's in the backyard," she said to me quickly. "Run around to the back and tell him Herbert's here and to come and say hello."

I skipped up the alley and burst into the backyard, and into my father's arms. He hugged me so hard I almost cried. He was bare to the waist, cutting dead branches off the peach tree. Drops of sweat ran down through the curls of dark hair on his chest.

"Mommy says to come and say hello to Herbert."

I pulled my father forward by the hand; he came slowly, letting me drag him toward the front of the house.

My mother had come down from the steps and was standing close beside Herbert. She seemed to stop talking suddenly as we came into view, and Herbert extended his hand to my father.

"You have no idea what a great pleasure it was to have your daughter with us this weekend."

My father shook Herbert's hand briefly, and my mother swayed to and fro, leaning on the pole of her dry mop. Herbert, hot and nervous in his tweed suit-jacket, shifted from one foot to another, saying his awkward good-byes. My father, who had bits of leaves and twigs in his thick black hair, looked around the yard, taking stock of the gardening he still needed to do. I saw that while I had been away, the popcorn-ball bush had bloomed into color.

When Herbert had driven off, my mother kissed me on the forehead and took my suitcase inside. I followed my father up the alley into the backyard and sat on the swing while he clipped branches off the peach tree with the rusted shears. My dog ran in circles around the yard like a maniac.

Once my father paused and looked over his shoulder at me.

"Glad to be home?"

In answer, I began to swing, grinning, and he stopped what he was doing to give me a magnificent push skyward.

The Mistress of Goldman's Antiques

In the past month I have frozen fourteen dinners in plastic margarine containers to bring to my mother. I should have labeled them when I froze them, but I am not an organized person.

My daughter Myra tells me that the cellophane tape won't stick to the cold covers and that the marking pen won't write on the wet plastic. I am rushed as it is, since the two older girls are already waiting in the car, but I run to the garage to find some masking tape in case it is stickier.

My husband, Danny, is in the driveway putting water in the radiator, and I call instructions to him over my shoulder while I hunt for the tape. "Put four folding chairs in the car, and the bag of oranges, and the carton of groceries. The milk and the hamburger meat are already in the ice chest. Don't forget the vacuum cleaner. My mother's is broken, and I told her I'd bring mine."

I rush back to the kitchen and we try the masking tape, which sticks to the round, translucent margarine lids better than the cellophane tape. I open each container and look at the icy stuff inside. "Write beef and barley soup on this one. Spaghetti and meat sauce on these two."

Myra is in the fourth grade and does not write too fast. I wait, and feel the pounding of my heart. I really don't want to go on this ride today. The truth is there's usually nothing much to say when we get to my mother's, since I talk to her for a half-hour on the phone every day. Her voice is still young, and she's usually cheerful on the phone. It's different when we go to see her.

"I'm ready, go ahead," Myra says. She pushes her hair out of her eyes and stares at me. Will she do this for me when I am a widow living alone in a two-room apartment?

"Write chicken soup and matzo balls on that one and the one beside it; this looks like beef stew in here. These three are brisket and kasha. The next two lasagna. Then cream cheese pie, noodle pudding, and banana-nut muffins."

My daughter completes the job with a grave air of responsibility. I tell her how important it is, and I thank her.

On the way to Los Angeles we pass the cemetery where my father is buried. We never used to go this way, but the new freeway makes the hour trip to my mother's a little shorter. We drive by the hill where my father has lain for ten years—he's a little to the left of some tall pine trees, and just below a trash can set in what looks to be the hollowed-out trunk of a tree. I remember the day my sister and I went shopping for a grave site. My mother could not leave my father's side at the City of Hope, and we knew we had to buy a plot immediately. We were giddy, listening to all the sales speeches about comfort and quiet and security, and we turned down sites in several cemeteries because we felt they were too noisy or unscenic or too crowded. We finally took this plot on top of the hill because the grass was green and the view was good, and because a bridle path ran along the bottom of the hill where young people rode beautiful horses. "Daddy would enjoy this," my sister said.

Now that the freeway is in, my father can enjoy the millions of cars, too. Sooner or later one will come along and his family will be in it. I wonder if he feels any special vibration when his blood kin zip by at fifty-five miles an hour. Since we usually come this way on Saturday, when the cemetery is closed, Danny always says that if I want to, we'll come back soon and visit the grave. For me, passing on the road is quite enough. All I would do if we drove onto the grounds would be to press my hand on the raised letters of the bronze plaque that has my father's name on it, and think about what the dead can know. As it is, I am left with a quiver in my stomach and a shiver down my back.

"If any of the rest of you are alive when I die," Myra says suddenly from the back of the station wagon, "I want to be buried in the grave-yard on Mesa Boulevard, right near our house."

"By the time you die," I say, "you may want to be buried far away, maybe in another state, maybe beside your husband or in his family plot. Or maybe Daddy and I ought to buy up all the land around my father, and then we can all be buried together."

"No," Myra says, "I want to stay near my home. My childhood was there." She is nine years old.

Luckily, the next attraction down the road is Universal Studios, and Danny turns the talk to the parting of the Red Sea, and the glacier that melts, and the size of the shark's teeth used in the "Jaws" movie.

The two older girls are reading books in the back seat; they are bored by these trips, and soon they will refuse to come. Last month it became clear that we did not all have to go to the same places at the same times anymore. It came about when Danny and I offered to take them all to see a Woody Allen movie if they got their rooms in shape first. As we were about to leave, I checked their rooms and found Bonnie's in complete disorder, clothes on the chair, pajamas kicked under the bed, books open underfoot, candy wrappers, knots of hair, high school hall passes, crumpled tissues on her dresser.

"Don't you want to go?" I said.

"Yes."

"But you didn't straighten your room."

"I guess not," she said.

"Then you can't go."

She shrugged.

"Then we'll all have to stay home because of you," I said.

"I can't help it."

"But your sisters cleaned their rooms in good faith. They want to go badly. What kind of a person are you?"

She shrugged.

In the end, with bitter anger between us, we left her home, alone, for the afternoon. As we walked out she and I looked at each other with fear. We had never left her alone before, under circumstances like this.

I said, "Please don't do anything drastic."

She ran to me and hugged me awkwardly, roughly, beginning to cry, and said, "I'm not that type. Don't worry."

Now she and Jill are reading adult books — novels. They get them in the library; I don't have anything to say about their reading anymore. They're mature girls for fourteen and twelve. Myra doesn't like to read. Of the three of them, she's the only one who listens to rock music for hours in her bedroom, and plays solitaire while her long bare toes tap the beat.

A car cuts in front of Danny and he stops short. I hear the cooler tip over and then the ice cubes slide across the floor.

"Stand the milk carton up straight before it spills," I shout to the girls in the back.

"Isn't it dumb to bring a quart of milk all the way to Mom-mom's?" Myra says.

"You know the reason," I say. "Mom-mom doesn't shop very much, and if I don't bring it, we don't have anything to drink there all evening."

As we drive through Hollywood we pass the Institute of Oral Love. We see a man walking down the street wearing a white lace midriff and carrying a flowered shoulder bag. Another man wearing a black cape and black boots, carrying a cage with a parrot in it, is waiting at a bus stop.

"Why do some men look like women?" Myra asks. I promise myself I'll talk to her about this another time, but now I cut her off firmly.

"Well, we're almost there and we must decide right now what we're going to do. Daddy has to get some books from the library at UCLA. He'll be back at Mom-mom's by dinnertime. We can let him drop us off at Mom-mom's store and we can spend the afternoon there, or we can wait at her apartment and you can play cards, or we can borrow Mom-mom's car and go to the Tar Pits and the County Museum. *Or* we could stop up and see Aunt Gert."

No one answers me. We have done each of those things so many times, they don't even bother to hear me.

I say to Danny, "Stop in the driveway at my mother's apartment first, so I can put the food in the freezer."

The old man who lives upstairs thinks there has been a tragedy as he comes down and sees the line of us standing at her door, with chairs, a vacuum cleaner, cartons, and bags.

"Mrs. Goldman died? Are you the new tenants?" he asks, as I struggle to choose from my keychain the various keys to the bolts my mother had installed after she was burglarized last year.

"No, she's fine. I'm her daughter. We're just visiting."

The old man clears his throat, then spits in the alley. He walks away. He and my mother are mortal enemies. He's deaf, and he listens to his TV at full volume. He also goes to the bathroom ten times a night — my mother hears his clumping about and has complained. They have both wished the other to drop dead, aloud, many times.

Danny and I exchange a glance. Even now the sound of too many neighbors, too close, is unbearable to us. We can smell onions and garlic frying, a child is screaming, dog turds are on the step in front of the mailboxes.

I get the door open and we carry in the folding chairs (my mother's dining table has only two chairs at it), the food I am going to cook for dinner, the frozen dinners which will nourish my mother for the next couple of weeks on the nights she is too tired or depressed to eat out, the cans of soup, and the oranges from our tree.

A man appears suddenly at the screen door, shouting and cursing. It seems that Danny's car is blocking the driveway. This is the Israeli hairdresser who lives in the building. He can't get by us to pull into his parking cubicle behind the building.

Danny steps outside, explaining to the man that there was no place to park on the street and we were just taking a few minutes to unload. He smiles and holds up his hand. No problem, he'll get his car out immediately. The dark-haired man is shouting in a language we recognize from having heard it in holy places — synagogues — but we have never heard such violence in it.

I tell the children to wait in the car with Daddy; quickly, in the dark little kitchen, I place the margarine containers one upon the other in the freezer. Nothing but half a loaf of white bread is in it. I wheel the vacuum cleaner into the bedroom. The space in the room is consumed by the king-size bed my mother and father used to share.

On the bed is their old pink electric blanket, which only warms on one side now. The TV is beside the bed (there is another one in the other room, on a bookcase) and the single window in the room is banded by iron bars. ("Would I rather die trapped in a fire, or be killed by a rapist?" my mother once asked me.)

I feel as if I am suffocating in this place. The windows — two in the whole apartment — are always kept heavily draped, for privacy, for safety. There is no air, no light, it is like a hole. No wonder my mother cannot cook in this place. It's a wonder she can breathe here.

In the living room I stop to play a few notes on the grand piano. It's the same one we had in Brooklyn when I was growing up; I used to practice my scales on it. On an impulse I go around to the side of it and look into one of the holes on the soundboard. When I was a child, my mother used to keep money hidden there, and her one fine bracelet made of gold lions' heads which my father gave her the first year he was in the antique business. Now there is a long envelope folded and crunched into the hole. I pull it out and recognize the drawing of Moses which is the symbol of the memorial park where my father is buried. I open the envelope and find the deed to a burial plot. My mother has bought herself a place on that hill beside my father without telling any of us.

I replace the envelope, get my purse, and carefully lock all the deadbolts with the proper keys. Then I run down the alley to the car, and Danny drives us the two blocks to the store.

The same battered yellow sign is there — my maiden name in lights — Goldman's Antiques. The buzzer shrills as we cross the threshold. It's a horrible sound, and always scares customers as they come in. My mother had it installed last year after she was surprised by a nun who ran out the door with a pair of candlesticks under her cape before my mother was aware someone had even entered the store. She'd been playing the upright piano in the back, which she often did when there was no business, which was most of the time.

The children love to stand in front of the electric eye and make the buzzer shriek. I can't stand the din. I scream at them to stop.

I kiss my mother. Half of her face is covered by immense, dark sunglasses, worn to keep the glare out of her sensitive eyes, which are not seeing very well these days.

She smiles at me. It's a funny, sorrowful smile, as if coming from a tearful face. She seems thinner than the last time I saw her. Her wispy hair is pure white and lies softly on her delicate head. Her face is like sunlight to me — I cannot look at it too long. It shocks my eyes, the way it has changed. I don't know how to reconcile my two mothers — the one with the radiant smile who used to wait for me with arms outstretched at the school gate when I was in first grade, and this present, mourning mother of mine, whose face has diminished to a wrinkled puff of air.

I turn my head away, grateful to hear her voice. It is the same as always, very vibrant, lilting, almost girlish.

"And how are my darling girls?" she says, embracing my children, who hug her back. She never kisses Danny, because she understood long ago that it is not his way.

I look around the shop. It is long and narrow, overcrowded, dense with things that curl and twist, everything is ornate, nothing is clean and straight, the way I like it. There are things here that Danny admires, that he would like to have in our home, but I refuse. Now that I have a choice, I want modern things, pure straight surfaces, smooth heavy planks of wood for tables, utilitarian objects, like clocks or lamps, which also serve as decorations.

I am terrified by the thought that someday soon all these objects will fall to me and my sister, be ours to dispose of. If I ever pray, I pray that my mother will choose to liquidate the shop while she is well and capable. There must be ten thousand items here in which I have absolutely no interest, whose value I cannot conceive of, whose dusty features repel me. But there is no doubt that my mother will keep this place going till the day she can no longer stand on her feet, and that will be the time (when she can't even help us) that my sister and I will become the unwilling recipients of this empire.

Even though my mother has for years made no profit from the store (and is lucky if her income barely covers her expenses), I know that this shop is what gets her out of bed in the morning, gets her dressed and into the world of the living. Here Anna Goldman has authority, she is in control. She meets people, she makes deals. She is the mistress of Goldman's Antiques. At home, in the dark hole she lives in, she is as good as in the ground with my father.

I wonder how I could have lived in my family so long and never learned to tell cut glass from pressed glass, silver from tin, diamonds from rhinestones. In this store my mother speaks a strange language to the ladies from Beverly Hills: "Tiffany," "Lalique," "Sonora Chimes," "Soapstone."

When, now and then, she comes to our home for the weekend, and I go on Sunday morning calls with her, I cringe as she makes offers to people who are forced to sell their beloved belongings because of death, or divorce, or deportation to old-age homes. She stands hard as a rock amid their dishes and silver and paintings and offers paper money for the accumulations of a lifetime.

I feel claustrophobic here, I must have air.

I shoot through the buzzer and stand outside, breathing hard. Danny is saying he has to get to the library before it closes, and my mother is telling him about this week's movie stars — how Barbra Streisand chiseled down the price of a beaded dress till my mother lost patience; how Red Skelton sent his chauffeur in to price a painting, lest my mother mark it up instantly when she recognized the comedian; how Glen Campbell was in and my mother didn't know him from a hole in the wall till the secretary who works next door came rushing in to breathe the air that had passed through his lungs.

It is going to be a very long afternoon. There are no chairs that aren't too fragile to sit on in the store, and the children have nothing to do. They knock into tables full of china, they touch things that are breakable, and they sometimes ask to have things.

"This is a place of business," my mother is now saying to Myra, hugging her to make refusal seem less cruel. "If I give my grandchildren all the things they want, I'll have nothing left to sell, isn't that true?"

Myra runs out to me and whispers, "I hate it here."

"What was it you wanted?" I ask her.

She takes me back through the buzzer, holding my hand. She points to a carved wooden dog, about an inch long, in the display case. I want to tell her that when the store is mine, she can have anything she wants. Everything, in fact. What harm could be done if my mother gave her that? Or ten or twenty other things as well? Would the family fortunes be diminished in any appreciable way?

"How about we walk over to Aunt Gert's?" I suggest. "Or since Daddy is leaving now, he could drop us off there."

"Yes, yes," Jill says, showing the first signs of life all day. "She makes the most delicious chocolate and vanilla mandelbrot."

"Bonnie?"

Bonnie shrugs. I know what she is thinking. Aunt Gert will comment on how nicely her bosom is coming along, and will question her about how often she washes her face and whether she is using the smelly acne soap Gert recommended as a charm against a ruined girlhood.

"We really should stop by," I say. "She'd feel very bad if she knew we were in LA and didn't drop in."

My mother agrees. "Gert always says she especially moved to California to be near my children. It wouldn't be nice not to go over."

What Aunt Gert always says to *me* is that she moved to California to be near my *mother* in order to see that she got a good meal inside her once in a while. We file out of the shop in staccato beeps, telling my mother to expect us back within the hour.

Aunt Gert knows Danny does not like to be kissed — I have had to tell her so — which means that when we come into her apartment, she doesn't kiss him, but says to him, standing an inch away, "If I didn't know you didn't like to be kissed, I'd kiss you, but since I know you don't, I won't."

That's enough for Danny. Politely, but very quickly, he departs and is finally on his way to the library.

"Aah," Aunt Gert says, kissing me. "It's so good to have my little babies here." She strokes Myra's cheek. "Soft as a baby's tush," she says. "And Bonnie, darling, you're getting such a shape, the boys will be knocking down the door soon."

Bonnie sends me a look of misery so acute that I remind myself to tell her about the Christmas I was in graduate school when I spent a week with Aunt Gert just after she was widowed. I slept on the hide-a-bed in the living room, and the first morning I awoke there, I heard Aunt Gert calling to me from the bedroom. "Come, darling, come in here and let's snuggle together like in the olden days." I was twenty-two years old then.

"Do you think you could stay in LA till ten or eleven tonight?" Aunt Gert asks. "I'd like you to come to a meeting — Harry and I are going to get an award tonight from the City of Hope for raising more than $2,000 this year. I'd like you to see that all this running around I do isn't for nothing."

"Oh, I know it's wonderful work you're doing, Aunt Gert. It's just that we'd get home after midnight, and that's too late for the children. Did you ask Mother to go with you?"

"Your mother! Of course I asked her, I always ask her. But when I told her the program is going to be a paramedic teaching the methods of, how do you call it, cardio-heart-massage, which is such a valuable thing to know at our age, what did your mother say? . . . she said, 'What do I need it for? To do it on myself, alone, someday in my apartment, when I have my heart attack?' Why is she like that? I offer her meetings, I offer her picnics, donor lunches, nothing is good enough for her. She goes nowhere. Only if someone is musical, a person is worth her time. I could have found her ten husbands since Abram died, he should rest in peace, but she won't be agreeable to meet men. Ten years ago she was still a good-looking woman, her skin was firm. Now look at her. She doesn't eat. Who would have her?"

"I don't think she's thinking about marriage," I say. "She's still missing Daddy too much."

"So I miss Clark Gable! But a practical marriage is something else. Harry never takes me anyplace I want to go — I would love to take a ride in the country and see the cows. But he likes my cooking, and he's generous to a fault. I'm grateful every day I was lucky to find a second husband so late in life. God should let him live a long time."

"Sometimes Mother prefers her own company. She gets a lot of pleasure from her music."

"Music! Can you hug a piano in bed?"

The girls are eating mandelbrot at a table covered with one of Aunt Gert's immaculate embroidered cloths.

"Are the *kinder* still lighting candles on Friday night?"

The girls all look at me. I am the leader of the conspiracy—Aunt Gert gave us Harry's dead mother's brass candlesticks on the condition we light Sabbath candles in them. We don't. That is the conspiracy.

"We try to remember," I say.

"I have coupons for you," she says. She goes to a drawer and takes out a bag of papers. She hands the valuables to me one by one, so I can appreciate them. Five cents off on oatmeal flakes, seven cents off on toilet paper, forty cents off on coffee, a one-dollar refund if I send six proof-of-purchase seals and the price labels from a pound of fudge cookies, plus the side of a carton of a half-gallon of acidophilus milk.

I nod, thank you, thank you. Danny says I am crazy—I should simply say I have no time for such nonsense. I don't need this junk; I can clip these out of my own newspaper if I want to. It's no *present*. But I smile. "How nice," I say. Then she gives me a little framed Sioux Indian prayer: "Great Spirit, grant that I may not criticize my neighbor until I have walked a mile in his moccasins." Then a poem called "The Value of a Smile," and a few clippings from the *Reader's Digest*—"Quotable Quotes," "Laughter Is the Best Medicine." My spiritual future is assured.

"Now I want five dollars from *you*," she says. "A raffle. You could win a trip to Israel."

By now I am prepared for this, and I pay her the money. I don't mind the raffle so much—it's when she tries to sell me and the children things we don't want that I get angry. "These are darling blue jeans, donated for the rummage sale by a very fancy store. They're just the right size for Myra. I'm only asking three dollars. In the store you'd pay fifteen."

"Myra wouldn't wear them. They have tapered leges. They're an old style, Aunt Gert."

"*Two* dollars, then."

"Well, girls," I say. "Time to walk back to the store. Mom-mom is waiting for us."

"You're walking?" Aunt Gert says. "In *this* neighborhood?"

"It's the middle of the day; nothing is going to happen."

"You don't know what's been going on here these days. A woman I know was raped in her own parking garage. Another old lady who lives next door, she's eighty-five, for six dollars in her purse they do a thing like that, knock her down, break her hip."

"We'll be careful," I promise. The girls put their glasses in the sink. Here, where everything is neat, they feel constrained. I would like to show them Aunt Gert's drawers as I recall them from my childhood. Every handkerchief was ironed into a perfect triangle, every lace slip without a wrinkle. Even now she irons her sheets. "They're perfectly good, they'll last another fifty years, what do I need this permanent press for, I have good linens."

We kiss good-bye. "Give me a vitamin," she tells each child. "Every kiss is a vitamin." She is too trusting to see the disdain in my daughters' faces. I feel a pang of guilt that I have raised such skeptics.

We are so happy to be out in the sunshine that the four of us hold hands wherever the street is wide enough, and we skip the six blocks to the antique store, giggling and laughing till we can hardly breathe.

The door to the shop is locked. My mother is sitting at her desk with her hands covering her face. My heart turns over. Is she sick? What is it?

I bang on the glass of the door.

Very slowly, she rises from her chair and walks to the door. It takes her a while to unlatch it. She leans against it, not quite letting us in.

"What's the matter? What is it, Ma?"

She tries to smile, but her lips are trembling. "I was held up," she says. "I was just held up."

Behind me I feel the children reach for each other.

"Are you all right? What happened? Here, let us in."

"I'm waiting for the police. It happened . . . not five minutes ago. He was in here. With a gun. He said he was going to kill me."

"Oh, God. I don't believe this."

We get inside and I lock the door behind us. We find seats; my mother does not notice that we're sitting on fine things, on embroidered satin chairs, on needlepoint stools.

"Tell me, Ma."

She is twisting the lion-head bracelet around and around on her wrist. The lions' ruby eyes look like drops of blood.

"I think Daddy saved my life," she said. "I've always felt he was keeping an eye on us. I don't know what happened. Something came into my mind, something made me say it."

"Say what?"

"I said, 'My husband will be back in ten minutes, he'll have more money with him.' "

"Ma, start at the beginning." Suddenly I ask myself if this would have happened if I'd stayed in the store with the children. What if we'd all been here? Danny could have come back from the library and found us all dead. I am filled with relief — and guilt for my gratitude — that we were not here. Then another dreadful thought comes to my mind — if worst had come to worst, my mother is, after all, almost seventy. Because I think that, I take both her hands in mine and kiss them. "Tell me."

"It happened a few minutes ago. I was playing the piano. I heard the buzzer. A young black man was in the front, maybe he was twenty. He had one of those knitted caps on his head. He said, 'What kind of wood is that table?' 'Fruitwood,' I said. I thought to myself, *What does a young boy like this need with an antique table that costs two hundred dollars?* But you never know these days. The richest stars come in here dressed like bums. And so many of the rock singers are black, who can tell who's a millionaire customer and who isn't? But then he took out his gun. 'Where's the money?' he said in a very low voice."

Myra starts to sob. I take her on my lap and kiss her face all over. "He won't come back again, darling," I tell her. "It's all right now. He probably wasn't a murderer. Maybe he was just hungry, maybe he had a family to feed. So many people have no jobs now."

"Don't defend him!" my mother shouts angrily. "He said, 'Get me the money or I'll kill you.' Don't have pity for him!"

A loud knock at the door makes us jump. But it's not the police, it's some woman who wants to come in.

I call out, "I'm sorry, we're closed now." The woman makes an ugly face through the glass and shakes her fist.

"Oh drop dead," my mother says. "They come in here and pester me day and night and they never buy anything. They say, 'You want twenty-five dollars for that piece of junk? My mother threw away ten just like it.' "

"Never mind, Ma. Tell me the rest now."

"There were no bills in the cashbox. When is the last time I made a sale? There were maybe twenty dollars worth of quarters. I put them all in a paper bag for him. He made me lift up the cashbox. There were four dollar bills under it. I handed them to him. He saw some broken gold pocket watches in the drawer, and he asked for them, too. Then he told me to get my purse."

"He took your purse?"

My mother half-smiles. "I'm not so dumb I haven't been expecting something like this. After all, an old woman alone in a fancy-looking store. Sooner or later it had to be me. So I keep a fake purse in the bottom drawer. With old eyeglasses in it, some keys to nothing, an old wallet with a ten-dollar bill. He made me hand him the money. He didn't want to touch anything. Then he said, 'Hold out your arm.' I didn't know what he was going to do to me. 'Give me that,' he said. He meant my lion-head bracelet. 'Oh, please don't take that,' I said. 'My husband gave that to me a long, long time ago.' I don't know why, but he didn't argue with me. But he was angry. 'Where's the rest of the money, then?' he said. And that's when I said, 'My husband will be back in ten minutes. He'll have more money with him.' It's as if Daddy put the words into my mouth. I know that scared him, he kept looking over his shoulder for Daddy to come in.

"Then he said, 'Get in the back.' He had the gun on my spine. He pushed me toward the bathroom, and came in it with me. He came *in with me,* Janet. I knew he was going to kill me then."

Now tears come to my mother's eyes. All my children start to cry with her, in terror. My mother stops crying and wipes her eyes. She laughs a little. "Look children —." She rolls up her sleeves, lifts her blouse halfway up her ribs. "No holes in me anywhere. I'm perfect — just like new. Nothing to cry about."

Jill jumps up and hugs her, still sobbing. Bonnie hugs her on top of Jill. They are all climbing over one another to feel that my mother is alive.

But she has to finish the story. It is forming now for posterity; I can hear my children telling it to their children. " 'If you make a sound I'll blow your head off,' he said. And then he left me there in the bathroom and closed the door. 'When can I come out?' I asked him. 'When I say so!' he said. And then I heard the buzzer, and I came out and saw he was gone, so I locked the door and called the police."

She looks around her. "So here I am."

We sit together, staring out front through the bars of the glass door. Finally my mother says, "I'm giving up the store, Janet. I've thought maybe it's time for quite a while, but now I know it's time. I can't take a chance and go through this again. Next time I may not be so lucky."

"But you *mustn't* give it up!" I say, now that my prayers are answered. "You need this place. You can't let one rotten criminal decide your whole future for you. A twenty-year-old kid! He's a nothing, a nobody! He can't be the one who decides you have to sit in your little apartment for the rest of your life."

"Other dealers are giving up. They're terrified. It happens up and down the street here, every day."

"You can't let bad people take over the world, Ma. You can't give in to terrorist tactics."

"You didn't see the gun, Janet."

"But don't decide today, while you can still feel the gun in your back. Give yourself some time."

"I suppose . . . maybe I could hire a security guard."

"Yes! Maybe you could."

"Or I could keep the door locked, and only let in people who look nice."

"Yes, maybe that's a way. . . . "

"I can't stay in that apartment. . . . "

Which is what I am thinking. "Of course you can't. You're much too active and energetic for that. If you give up the store, what would there be for you to do?"

"I could sell raffles for the City of Hope," she says bitterly.

Finally, a dramatic shadow appears at the door. A policeman has come. My mother is going to tell the story all over again. I see her getting her words in order.

I stand up. "I'll take the children back to your place, now, Mom. There's no room for all of us to stay here. I'll start dinner cooking."

"Oh no, I could never think of eating tonight."

"But I brought food. And chairs to sit on." She is unlocking the door for the policeman, who is tall and has curly brown hair. He is extraordinarily handsome in his uniform.

"If you and your family are hungry, you can go out to eat later," she says over her shoulder.

I start to argue but I have lost her. She is smiling up at the policeman as they walk to her desk. He is such a concerned and gentle man, and she is such a small and graceful and vulnerable woman.

From the front of the store I glance back. Her white hair could be auburn. She could be twenty years old. Her charming laugh to something reassuring he says is pure flirtation. The man there could be my father.

There is no way to get out the door without jumping to the jolt of the buzzer.

Memorial Service

A poster of Superman hung in the boys' room, the last remnant of their tenancy after my sister Carol had cleaned out their drawers and closets in a burst of manic energy. It was the day before Bard's "funeral." Although the cremation had already taken place, a service had been arranged by Bard's mother and sister. Carol was sick with a bad case of bronchitis which had been hanging on for weeks. She had said to me she didn't see why it was necessary to have some elaborate ritual to mourn her husband's passage from life when he had elected to kill himself.

I held back the flaps of a large carton for her as she tore shirts and jackets out of his closet in their bedroom and threw them into the box, letting the hangers clang on one another in a fierce racket. She was giving most of his clothes to the Salvation Army, saving only a few things — his London Fog raincoat and his Shetland wool sweater — because my daughter Myra had asked her to save them for her. The house was already listed for sale with a realtor; in two days it would be open to prospective buyers. She wanted to sell it fast, for money, so she would have something to live on while she figured out what to do.

Early this morning we had gone to an equipment-rental company near my house and walked among the tillers, backhoes, and earth movers till we found a white Ford van which seemed to be the right size. Two bearded young men behind the counter tried to flirt with Carol, one of them asking if she needed help moving, the other asking if she had any use whatsoever for an able-bodied man. She leaned her thin elbows on the counter beside a crinkled piece of black carbon paper and held her head in her hands. Her dark hair fell forward like a curtain around her face. Then she looked up at them and said, "Please, I don't have the strength for these games now."

"She has the flu," I explained, and, picking up the key to the van, took her arm and led her out to the parking lot.

She insisted on driving. She said she was too restless to sit still. In the back, her two boys slid about on the ridged metal floor, trying to anchor themselves. Our plan was to go through the house, take back to my garage what she wanted to keep, throw away the junk, and put price stickers on everything else she wanted to sell tomorrow morning at the yard sale, before the service. She had already placed an ad in the Sunday paper.

"Don't you think you're trying to do too much at once?" I had asked her as she drove the rattling van too fast along the freeway. She kept trying to take deep breaths. The boys were complaining that the floor of the van was dirty, that they had no soft place to rest their backs, that the smell of the exhaust was making them sick. I had a notebook on my lap; we were making lists of what she had to do. There were five pages of lists, having to do with the furniture sale, with the closing of utilities and bank accounts, with paying off debts and bills. One page was a reminder to call the crematorium to make sure the ashes would be scattered at sea as specified the following Thursday. Another page had been set aside to list the kinds of work Carol thought she was qualified to do to support her family. The notations on that page read: "#1, Waitress; #2, Typist." I had idly scribbled Carol's remark when she couldn't think of a #3: *God help me, I'm not prepared for this.*

"How could I be doing too much?" she asked. "I mean, after this last week, what could be too much? If I could live through that, I can live through anything." She tried to breathe. "I think I'm hyperventilating," she said. "I hope I don't faint and kill us all." She laughed. "Or maybe that would make it convenient. After all, his mother and sister reserved the church already, his mother is flying down, and Mom and Aunt Gert and Uncle Harry will be there, and Bard's two friends, Clint, the junkie, and his buddy the drug dealer, so we could get it all over with at once." She changed lanes without signaling, cutting the wheels sharply, so that the boys rolled against each other in the back. "To make it a real party I could have invited all the women from the shelter. They'd arrive with balloons and little party hats to celebrate."

"Are you that bitter?"

"No, I'm not bitter. I'm grateful to them, I think. But you know their policy, no sympathy for the batterer. A dead husband is one less crazy man in the world to deal with. They don't believe in crying over it. They say it's sometimes a blessing in disguise." She gave the van more gas. "I never got as tough as they wanted me to get. I just could never say good riddance and walk away. I loved him too much. They couldn't indoctrinate me quite to that point."

"Hey Mom, will you *watch* it?" Abram, the oldest boy, called in alarm. "You just cut off that BMW."

"Can you believe it?" Carol said to me. "His mother and sister arranged for the church, the minister, the organist, they probably ordered flowers, and they're billing *me!*"

"As far as they're concerned, you owe them an eternal debt because Regina picked up Bard's car from the police station. At least, that's how it sounded that afternoon when Regina finally called me. She made it clear that it was the worst ordeal of her life, driving Bard's car back to your house, having to breathe in the fumes that were left in it."

"Ugh," Carol said, and shuddered. "The Volvo. I never want to see that car again. He kept the vacuum cleaner hose in it all the time. I never understood why. How could I have guessed what he was planning to do with it?"

"You'll want to sell the car, too," I said, adding it as an item on the list of things for sale.

"Make a new list," she said. "Title it *Memorial Service*." She turned her head and called above the noise of the engine to her sons: "Think of some things you want to say about Daddy. You'll need to say some things about him at the funeral tomorrow. Janet will write them down. Tell her how you feel about all this."

"I don't want to say *anything,*" Abram said.

"*I'll* tell you how I feel!" David, her younger son, screamed from the back. "I hate everything. I hate this truck; it's hard as a rock and noisy and it stinks here."

"And *I* don't want to move away! What about our backyard?" Abram demanded. "What about my treehouse, and my fort? What about Mike and my other friends?"

"We'll all have to make adjustments," Carol called to him over her shoulder. "Some things we just won't have from now on. And we won't make a fuss about it, either. Do you understand me? We aren't going to make any fusses."

Superman stood six-feet tall on the boys' bedroom wall, which was smudged with fingerprints and crayon lines. In his red cape and blue tights, his yellow belt and jockey shorts, he stood guard—his fists clenched, a single lock of hair falling forward on his handsome forehead—beside a window that looked out onto the foliage of the backyard. Strawberry plants with their red fat berries were creeping out of the pots in which Bard had planted them. Oleanders were in bloom under the window. Bard had made himself a tea of oleander leaves one day a little more than a month ago. Carol had come home from the store and seen the stew of leaves bubbling on the stove. Bard sat at the kitchen table he'd built into the wall, stirring some of the mixture in a cup. He had been trying all that morning to convince Carol to agree to something (she couldn't remember what—one of his plans to sell the house and grow kiwi fruit in the desert, or open a worm farm in the mountains and raise bait-worms for fishing), and she had repeated her usual rational arguments. When she came home with her bags of groceries he was ready for her. He raised the cup and gulped down some of the tea.

"I don't believe you're doing this! Did you swallow the whole cup? Was it full?" she had demanded of him. The children had come in from the yard and were watching.

"What do you care?" he'd said. "Here—want some?"

She had taken him, then, to the emergency room of the hospital. He had seemed rather pleased with all the excitement.

"Just watch him," the doctor had said. "He probably hasn't had enough to do him much harm."

A few days after that, Bard tore that same kitchen table from its moorings, broke the legs from it, and threw it out into the backyard. Then he had bashed his head through the wall and bit his youngest son on the scalp.

While Carol was working in another part of the house, I knelt on my hands and knees and pulled the last of the coloring-book pages and toys from under the boys' beds. I found, among the dust puffs, two of the boys' metal hot cars, odd socks, pennies, jacks, and a red plastic death's head ring. I put them all into a yellow sand pail with a little painted shovel on it — as well as a rubber snake, a ball, and a set of red wax vampire's teeth.

"Jesus Christ!" Carol called, stomping down the hall toward me. "All Bard's things are gone from the garage! His fishing rods and his camping gear, his drills and saws, his Coleman stove, all his stuff!"

"Do you think he sold them or pawned them for food money those last few days?"

"No, I think his sister stole them."

Bard's sister Regina lived in Venice, a block from the beach, in a little wooden house that was splintered and battered by ocean wind. She had been an aspiring actress. Long ago she had had her nose and breasts improved to increase her chances at stardom, but now she was selling suitcases and imitation designer jeans imported from Taiwan at a little sidewalk booth on the Venice promenade.

"Oh Carol, *sweetie,*" she sighed as she opened the door for us, but she had trouble embracing Carol with her drink in one hand and her cigarette in the other.

Carol stepped back. "Would you mind putting that out?" she said. "I'm having trouble breathing as it is."

"Oh, you poor baby," she said. She took another long drag and threw her cigarette out the door, behind us. Then she came down the steps and ground it out with the toe of her wooden clog. Her legs, in cut-offs, were muscular and aggressive-looking.

"You have no idea what a nightmare it was," Regina said, pushing a hairpin into place in her blonde, messy bun, ". . . driving that car that he died in, sitting in that seat where he took his last breaths, my poor crazy brother, thinking his. . . ."

Carol cut her off. "I can't find his fishing rods. They weren't in the garage. Do you know where they are?"

"It was just lucky that he had my number in his wallet," Regina went on. "If he hadn't, God knows, he could have been just one more missing person in the morgue. Of course, if you hadn't been hiding away in that shelter for battered women, the police would have called *you,* which would have been the best thing. In fact, if you want to get right down to the nitty-gritty, if you hadn't been in the shelter he probably wouldn't have done it. But what's the difference? Maybe it was meant to be that I got the bad news first. That's how it worked out, and I didn't shirk my duty. You know *that,* Carol. And I couldn't sleep all that night. God, did I cry."

"You didn't call my sister till two days later," Carol said coldly.

"Well, the first night, I thought, like Mom always taught us, never tell anyone bad news at night, then they have the whole dark night to think about it. Never tell bad news till the sun is shining. . . ."

"That was the *first* night."

"Well, then the next day I called Mom, you know, and she nearly had a breakdown on the phone, so I had to keep her from killing herself—she's not the strongest person, you know. None of us are." Regina laughed a little wildly. "By the time I got her calmed down it was night again. You know how it is."

"He killed himself on Saturday, Regina," Carol said. "I didn't learn about it till Monday afternoon. You didn't call my sister till Monday afternoon."

"What's the difference?" Regina said. "Dead is dead. Are you all coming in?"

"Where are Bard's fishing rods?"

"You're just lucky they weren't stolen," Regina said, leading us into her living room, motioning for us to sit on her tattered couch. "Hey, boys, you want some grape juice or something? Just help yourselves in the kitchen."

"They don't need anything," Carol said. "Not only the fishing rods are gone, along with Bard's drills and his camping gear. A coatrack we bought at Bamboo Imports a few months ago, it was right inside the front door. That's gone."

David, who had disappeared down the hall, called out, "Hey, it's in here, in the bedroom, Mom."

Regina and Carol looked at each other.

"Look, Carol," Regina said, "Bard told us you were gone for good, that's what he told Mom and me. He said they were teaching you how to hate him in that shelter, that they were brainwashing you and he didn't have a chance, and anything we wanted we could have because he wasn't going to need it."

"He told you that? To come into the house and take our things?"

"Well, he said if he took off we could have anything we needed."

"Took off?"

"He said he might take off for good, to the Kentucky hills or somewhere, that he just couldn't live around here anymore without you and the boys."

"You *needed* his drills and his fishing rods?"

"Well, Mom wanted those. I shipped them up to her."

"You took them out of my house? When? The instant you got the call from the police?"

"I didn't think you were coming back."

"How did you get in?"

"How? Through the door, that's how! Because when my poor brother ran out to kill himself he didn't bother to lock the door. Maybe he wasn't thinking about your coatrack just then. He just left the front door wide open. He left his note to you on the floor, just inside the door."

"HIS NOTE?"

Regina took a cigarette from the box on the coffee table and lit it with trembling fingers.

Carol's voice was wild with threat. "*What note did he leave? Where is it? Why wasn't I told about it?*"

"It was nothing," Regina said. "All it said, more or less, was 'I can't live without you and the boys.' That's all."

"Get it for me," Carol said. "I want it."

"Mom has it. I sent it up to her with the other stuff I shipped up. After all, he was her only son."

"I don't believe this," Carol said. She swayed toward me, leaned against the wall, tried to take a deep breath. She coughed, a rough, rattling sound that curled up through her lungs. She had trouble catching her breath.

"Get Mommy a drink from the kitchen," I said to Abram, who was standing at his mother's side. "Water."

"Oh, hey," Regina said, "let's not fight at a time like this. You can have anything back that you want. I just brought a lot of stuff over here for safekeeping so no one would steal it, and I sent some of it up to Mom in case she could find some consolation in having his things around. You know how she worshiped him."

"When is she arriving? It has to be soon, doesn't it, if the funeral service is tomorrow?"

"I'm meeting her tomorrow morning at the airport," Regina said.

"Then call her tonight and tell her to bring me his note. I haven't seen it. I didn't even know that he left me a note. It belongs to me and I want it."

"Call her? Tomorrow is Mother's Day, Carol. I hate to upset her any further. She's suffering enough. Couldn't it wait?"

Abram came into the living room. "Aunt Regina has our oak candlesticks, Mom," he said. "And our folding stepladder. And she has our wine glasses that Daddy bought in Mexico. They're in her cabinet." He held out a glass of water to Carol. "Here, I brought you your drink in one of them, so you can feel at home."

"Let's see if there's anything here I can't live without," said a big red-faced man in a cowboy hat, stepping among the objects for sale on Carol's front lawn.

"Can you use a car? . . . cheap?" Carol asked.

The Volvo was parked at the curb, where Regina had left it the Saturday night she had picked it up from the police station. Bard had been found in it, dead. Earlier that Saturday he had called me to say that if Carol didn't call him back from the shelter in ten minutes, he was checking out forever. He had driven the Volvo into the parking structure of a big singles complex, apparently in obedience to Carol's request that if he had to kill himself, to please not do it in the house where she might come in and find him. A tenant had discovered him on the upper level of the parking structure, near some stored sail-boats, slumped over in his seat, the vacuum cleaner hose connected from the exhaust pipe to just inside the back window.

"How cheap?"

"Oh, God, I don't know. Five hundred dollars? My husband just put in a new motor and transmission that cost over fifteen hundred."

"So why doesn't he want to keep it?"

"They're getting a divorce," I said to the man, moving over the grass toward the car. "Do you want to look at it?"

He opened the driver's door and leaned in. "Smells funny," he said. "Looks dusty. What is all this soot on the windows, anyway?"

"It's a good car," I said. I began to cough. I wondered what they had done with the vacuum cleaner hose. There was still a towel in the back seat. Had he used that to plug the window opening where the hose came in?

"Naah," the man said, backing out. "I don't think so."

Out on the lawn, Carol was leaning on one of the four posters from the frame of her waterbed, talking to a young couple. She was talking very fast, her cheeks flushed. She had hired some neighbor-hood teenagers early this morning to move everything that she wanted to sell out to the lawn. "I don't want to keep any of this stuff," she said to me. "I don't want to sit on that couch again, touch that lamp again. It's over. It all goes."

She was coughing heavily.

"Are you okay?" I asked.

"Nothing that a little hemlock wouldn't cure," she said. She moved off, rushing around on the lawn, asking the Sunday morning buyers, "Do you like it? How much will you give me for it? I'll take anything reasonable. Even unreasonable. Just make me an offer." Now she came back and said to the couple, "You can have the waterbed for fifty dollars; we paid four hundred. It's in perfect condition. Go around to the backyard with my sister. The mattress is draining back there. She'll show it to you."

The couple followed me to the back. A translucent green hose, at-tached to the waterbed in the house and coming out through the sliding glass door, lay gleaming like an emerald snake in the sunlight on the wooden patio deck. A stream of water came flowing from it in irregular bursts. The water puddled in a dingy pool in the grass.

"Why is she selling it?" the girl said to me. Her hair was in braids; she was pregnant.

"Domestic difficulties," I said.

"Yeah, I know how that is. Well, we'll think about it, thank you," she said. "Sometimes, you know, for a bed, you'd like to start brand new."

"Well, good luck then," I said. When they had left, I went into the garage and began putting things in boxes — half-empty cans of paint, machine oil, screws, masking tape. Carol had said I should take home anything my husband might be able to use. I accidentally tipped a little bottle of gold glitter from the workbench; it scattered through the air like a sun exploding and clung to my black skirt and my black shoes. I had forgotten that I was dressed for a funeral. An aluminum film canister seemed about to tip off the shelf. I caught it in my hand and opened it. Inside, a thousand little seeds rattled against one another. Then I found a hundred-pound bag of pinto beans in the dark, cobwebby corner under the workbench. I put the film canister in my suit pocket and dragged the burlap sack to the front lawn.

"Look at this," I said to Carol. She was counting out a wad of bills.

"I sold everything," she said smiling. "They cheated me blind, but I don't care. What do I care? I'm rid of it. They're coming back in a truck to get it all in a half-hour. We're lucky, you know. We could have sold none of it." She coughed, holding her breasts. When she caught her breath she said, "Don't worry about me. It sounds bad but I'm actually getting better, it's breaking up."

"Look in here," I said, opening the burlap sack and letting her see the spotted beans, curled upon one another like nesting animals.

"Oh, yeah," she said. "*That* was going to save us when doomsday came. One day, when we didn't even have enough money to buy milk for the boys, he came in and said to me, 'How come we don't have an emergency supply of food? I feel like killing.' So he went out and bought that crap. It's probably still on his credit card. I'll probably get the bill for it next month."

"I think we ought to take it home in the van. It's good food. You could live on it for a year."

"God!" she said, turning on me angrily. "Who *knows* what kind of poison he sprayed on that? Who knows what he might have put into it? Maybe he was counting on my eating it. Then I would join him, just like he wanted me to, me and the boys. No, just *throw* it out, throw out all the food in the house!" She kicked the heavy bag of beans.

"Do you know what this is?" I asked, reaching into my pocket and holding out to her the canister of tiny seeds.

"Oh, that," she said. "That's probably the most valuable thing he owned, *prime sensimilla,* the best. His pride and joy. Do me a favor. Take all these seeds out in the back yard and scatter them to the winds. Give the birds something to be happy about. Let them have the peace he never could get from that stuff. Let someone have peace, because he sure couldn't. I sure can't."

Regina and her mother, both of them wiry women with bleached hair, entered the church uncertainly and then went to sit by themselves in an empty pew a few rows from the altar. Bard's mother took a large, flowered handkerchief from her purse and wiped her eyes. My mother and aunt, followed by my uncle, entered the church, their elbows linked, and looked over at the two blonde women, then took seats in the same row but at the opposite end, across the aisle. Our relatives had arrived separately, in two cars. My husband, my children, and Carol's sons in our car, and our mother, aunt, and uncle in Uncle Harry's car. As Carol had predicted, Bard's two friends, the junkie and the drug pusher, slouched in and sat in the back. ("I had to call them," Carol had explained to me. "You can't have a memorial service with no one there. It wouldn't be fair to Bard.")

The boys came to stand at their mother's side. They were dressed in sport jackets and dress shoes much too small for them, the best Carol had been able to unearth from the cartons we had brought back to my house in the van. The boys wore around their necks little silver sneakers on chains which they had been given by the art therapist at the battered women's shelter when they had lived there with their mother. Last night, before they went to sleep, we had finally composed a list of things they wanted to say about their father. They didn't want to say them aloud, so I promised that I would do it for them. Carol, holding each son by the hand, went to sit in the front pew. I sat in the row behind her with my family. My daughters, in their lacy, unfamiliar dresses, looked frozen. My husband took my hand and said, "Soon this will all be over and we'll try to get back to some normal kind of life."

Carol, in front of me in her dark blue suit, shook with a violent chill every few seconds. Behind me I could hear the whispers of my mother and aunt. I thought they were relieved that Bard had killed himself, since in their view he had never offered Carol anything but trouble and danger.

I remembered how he had sounded on that last day, begging me to have her call him. I remembered the letter he had sent me for her, which began, *Dear Carol, Oh please, Carol, give me strength, give me courage, give me love, give me light. I am so scared being so alone. I am not violent. I am ashamed, lonely and unhappy with my lot. Losing you is too much, nothing I could have done could deserve that punishment. . . .*

The organist began to play; a minister in a white robe came and stood behind the lectern. My Jewish mother and aunt whispered to one another, uneasy about being in a church. When I glanced back at them once, they were staring at Christ impaled on his cross of wood, a dark figure against the beacon of muted afternoon light coming through the stained-glass window.

The minister spoke about tortured souls, about peace which could be obtained only in heaven, about forgiveness and love. Carol's face was rapt, colored by the rainbow of light coming through the window. I had the sense that the empty church had filled, that a great throng of witnesses had arrived to take part. The minister promised that Bard was now free from earthly pain. I felt a tap on my shoulder, and reaching back, felt my mother take my hand and press it hard. I thought I should reach forward, for Carol's hand, but her attention was perfect and private. Even her children did not touch her. Then I heard my name called. I rose and walked carefully up the carpeted steps.

I unfolded my page of notebook paper on the lectern. "Here are some things," I said, "that Bard's sons said about him." I found myself looking at Bard's mother and sister. I was surprised that they did not look like villains or criminals. They were both crying. My mother was crying. My aunt and my daughters were crying. My husband looked somber and shocked.

"This is what Abram said about his father:

'He gave me happy feelings.

'He figured out hard things.

'Some of the things he liked to do with me were fishing, wrestling, and visiting. I wish he never had an illness. I wish I could have had him longer. I miss him a lot. I will always love him.'

"Here are some things David said about his father:

'He was a good dad to me.

'He took me fishing, he taught me how to build things out of wood, how to fix things, how to work on my bike; he taught me many things, like the times tables. I wish he had been a happier person and not so sick. I am sad that he will not see me grow up.' "

I stepped down from the altar, moved down along the carpeted stairs, and found that I was passing Bard's mother as she made her way up them.

"It's a terrible thing for a mother to outlive her son," she said. "My son was just too sensitive for this life. He couldn't take it like most of us do. I loved him, I adored him. And since he won't be around to see his sons grow up, I'll try to hang on as long as God lets me and be here if they ever need me." She glanced down at Carol. "I hope their mother will let me visit them sometimes." She paused for a long time, and looked at each one of us. "Well," she said finally, "I know Bard can hear me, so I'll say, 'Good-bye, son, no, not good-bye, just so long."

Outside, the ocean wind was cold. Carol was shivering. We all surrounded her, circled her, in our dark suits. Regina and Bard's mother stood hesitantly outside the circle till my mother stepped back and, putting her arms around their waists, drew them in. Bard's friend, Clint, said, "Hey, listen, let me buy you all some coffee." There was some murmuring about what to do. My husband suggested that we all go back to the house; he pointed out his car and invited everyone to follow him.

The furniture that had been on the lawn was all gone. A few boxes waited for pickup by the Salvation Army. Carol entered the empty house. She sat down on the green rug in front of the cold fireplace. Charcoal-black streaks stained the white brick mantel and a swirl of ashes blew up in a flurry of wind which came in the open front door.

Bard's friend Clint arrived with two dozen doughnuts and styrofoam cups full of steaming black coffee. For the children he had bought little wax cartons of milk. He had remembered straws and napkins. The doughnuts were incredibly sweet; flakes of sugar stuck to everyone's lips and fingers.

Bard's mother asked Carol if she could speak to her privately. Carol had trouble standing, so I helped her to raise herself to her feet and she walked with Bard's mother down the hall. From the living room I could see them standing in Carol and Bard's old bedroom, standing in the square on the rug where the four bedposts had made their indentations. Bard's mother produced a little box and handed it to Carol. I saw Carol accept the box. The two women whispered together. Carol put out her arms and the older woman stepped forward and came into them. They hugged awkwardly. Then, blowing her nose on her flowered handkerchief, Bard's mother hurried into the bathroom and closed the door.

I went back to join Carol. "She brought the note," Carol said. "And I'm giving her the Volvo. She wants it. She told me she always knew he'd do it someday. That he had a thin skin; that he wasn't tough enough for this world."

The boys ran through the bedroom and out the sliding glass door to the backyard for a final climb up to their tree house. Carol left me and wandered down the hall. When I went to look for her a little while later, I found her in the boys' room, standing before the poster of Superman, shaking like a pneumatic drill.

In the hospital emergency room, a nurse sat Carol in a wheelchair and said there would be a wait, they had a bad case coming in. Carol, vibrating in her monumental chill, tried to nod. I protested to the nurse that this, too, was an emergency, that my sister's fever was very high, that she had just come from her husband's funeral. When this special pleading did not move her, I whispered, "A suicide's funeral!"

But just then the automatic glass doors parted and three police officers in black uniforms helped two orderlies rush a gurney with a man on it through the waiting room.

"Motorcycle accident," someone said, in fearful awe. It was the nurse, standing beside me.

In a moment we heard screams coming from a distant room, the strangled sounds of a man crying, "Ma! Ma!"

Carol took my hand. At last she cried. "God," she said, "I hope he lives."

"I Don't Believe This"

After it was all over, one final detail emerged, so bizarre that my sister laughed crazily, holding both hands over her ears as she read the long article in the newspaper. I had brought it across the street to show it to her; now that she was my neighbor, I came to see her and the boys several times a day. The article said that the crematorium to which her husband's body had been entrusted for cremation, had been burning six bodies at a time, and dumping most of the bone and ash into plastic garbage bags which went directly into their dumpsters. A disgruntled employee had tattled.

"Can you imagine?" Carol said, laughing. "Even that! Oh, his poor mother! His poor *father!*" She began to cry. "I don't believe this," she said. That was what she had said on the day of the cremation when she sat in my backyard in a beach chair at the far end of the garden, holding on to a washcloth. I think she was prepared to cry so hard that an ordinary handkerchief would not do. But she remained dry-eyed. When I came outside after a while, she said, "I think of his beautiful face burning, of his eyes burning." She looked up at the blank blue sky and said, "I just don't believe this. I try to think of what he was feeling when he gulped in that stinking gas. What could he have been thinking? I know he was blaming me."

She rattled the newspaper. "A dumpster! Oh, Bard would have loved that. Even at the end, he couldn't get it right. Nothing ever went right for him, did it? And all along I've been thinking that I won't ever be able to swim in the ocean again, because his ashes are floating in it! Can you believe it? How that woman at the mortuary promised they would play Pachelbel's *Canon* on the little boat, and the remains would be scattered with 'dignity and taste'? His *mother* even came all the way down with that jar of his father's ashes that she had saved for thirty years, so father and son could be mixed together for all eternity. Plastic garbage baggies! You know," she said, looking at me, "life is just a joke, a bad joke, isn't it?"

Bard had not believed me when I'd told him that my sister was in a shelter for battered women. Afraid of *him?* Running away from *him?* The world was full of dangers from which only *he* could protect her! He had accused me of hiding her in my house. "Would I be so foolish?" I had said. "She knows it's the first place you'd look."

"You better put me in touch with her," he had said menacingly. "You both know I can't handle this for long."

It had gone on for weeks. On the last day he called me three times, demanding to be put in touch with her. "Do you understand me?" he threatened me. "If she doesn't call here in ten minutes, I'm checking out. Do you believe me?"

"I believe you," I said. "But you know she can't call you. She can't be reached in the shelter. They don't want the women there to be manipulated by their men. They want them to have space and time to think."

"Manipulated?" He was incredulous. "I'm checking *out,* this is *IT.* Goodbye forever!"

He hung up. It wasn't true that Carol couldn't be reached. I had the number. I had not only been calling her, but I had also been playing tapes for her of his conversations over the phone during the past weeks. This one I hadn't taped. The tape recorder was in a different room.

"Should I call her and tell her?" I asked my husband.

"Why bother?" he said. He and the children were eating dinner; he was becoming annoyed by this continual disruption in our lives. "He calls every day and says he's killing himself and he never does. Why should this call be any different?"

Then the phone rang. It was my sister. She had a fever and bronchitis. I could barely recognize her voice.

"Could you bring me some cough syrup with codeine tomorrow?" she asked.

"Is your cough very bad?"

"No, it's not too bad, but maybe the codeine will help me get to sleep. I can't sleep here at all. I just can't sleep."

"He just called."

"Really," she said. "What a surprise!" But the sarcasm didn't hide her fear. "What this time?"

"He's going to kill himself in ten minutes unless you call him."

"So what else is new?" She made a funny sound. I was frightened of her these days. I couldn't read her thoughts. I didn't know if the sound was a cough or a sob.

"Do you want to call him?" I suggested. I was afraid to be responsible. "I know you're not supposed to."

"I don't know," she said. "I'm breaking all the rules anyway."

The rules were very strict. No contact with the batterer, no news of him, no worrying about him. Forget him. Only female relatives could call, and they were not to relay any news of him—not how sorry he was, not how desperate he was, not how he had promised to reform and never do it again, not how he was going to kill himself if she didn't come home. Once I had called the shelter for advice, saying that I thought he was serious this time, that he was going to do it. The counselor there—a deep-voiced woman named Katherine—said to me, very calmly, "It might just be the best thing; it might be a blessing in disguise."

My sister blew her nose. "I'll call him," she said. "I'll tell him I'm sick and to leave you alone and to leave me alone."

I hung up and sat down to try to eat my dinner. My children's faces were full of fear. I could not possibly reassure them about any of this. Then the phone rang again. It was my sister.

"Oh, God," she said. "I called him. I told him to stop bothering you, and he said, '*I have to ask you one thing, just one thing, I have to know this. Do you love me?*' " My sister gasped for breath. "I shouted *No*—what else could I say? That's how I *felt,* I'm so sick, this is such a nightmare, and then he just hung up. A minute later I tried to call him back to tell him that I didn't mean it, that I did love him, that I *do,* but he was gone." She began to cry. "He was gone."

"There's nothing you can do," I said. My teeth were chattering as I spoke. "He's done this before. He'll call me tomorrow morning full of remorse for worrying you."

"I can hardly breathe," she said. "I have a high fever and the boys are going mad cooped up here." She paused to blow her nose. "I don't believe any of this. I really don't."

Afterward she moved right across the street from me. At first she rented the little house, but then it was put up for sale and my mother and aunt found enough money to make a down payment so she could be near me and I could take care of her till she got her strength back. I could see her bedroom window from my bedroom window — we were that close. I often thought of her trying to sleep in that house, alone there with her sons and the new, big watchdog. She told me that the dog barked at every tiny sound and frightened her when there was nothing to be frightened of. She was sorry she had gotten him. I could hear his barking from my house, at strange hours, often in the middle of the night.

I remembered when she and I had shared a bedroom as children. We giggled every night in our beds and made our father furious. He would come in and threaten to smack us. How could he sleep, how could he go to work in the morning, if we were going to giggle all night? That made us laugh even harder. Each time he went back to his room, we would throw the quilts over our heads and laugh till we nearly suffocated. One night our father came to quiet us four times. I remember the angry hunch of his back as he walked, barefooted, back to his bedroom. When he returned the last time, stomping like a giant, he smacked us, each once, very hard, on our upper thighs. That made us quiet. We were stunned. When he was gone, Carol turned on the light and pulled down her pajama bottoms to show me the marks of his violence. I showed her mine. Each of us had our father's handprint, five red fingers, on the white skin of her thigh. She had crept into my bed, where we clung to each other till the burning, stinging shock subsided and we could sleep.

Carol's sons, living on our quiet adult street, complained to her that they missed the shelter. They rarely asked about their father and occasionally said they wished they could see their old friends and their old school. For a few weeks they had gone to a school near the shelter; all the children had to go to school. But one day Bard had called me and told me he was trying to find the children. He said he wanted to take them out to lunch. He knew they had to be at some school. He was going to go to every school in the district and look in every classroom, ask everyone he saw if any of the children there looked like his children. He would find them. "You can't keep them from me," he said, his voice breaking. "They belong to me. They love me."

Carol had taken them out of school at once. An art therapist at the shelter held a workshop with the children every day. He was a gentle, soft-spoken man named Ned, who had the children draw domestic scenes and was never once surprised at the knives, bloody wounds, or broken windows that they drew. He gave each of them a special present, a necklace with a silver running-shoe charm, which only children at the shelter were entitled to wear. It made them special, he said. It made them part of a club to which no one else could belong.

While the children played with crayons, their mothers were indoctrinated by women who had survived, who taught the arts of survival. The essential rule was: *Forget him, he's on his own, the only person you have to worry about is yourself.* A woman who was in the shelter at the same time Carol was had had her throat slashed. Her husband had cut her vocal cords. She could only speak in a grating whisper. Her husband had done it in the bathroom with her son watching. Yet each night she sneaked out and called her husband from a nearby shopping center. She was discovered and disciplined by the administration; they threatened to put her out of the shelter if she called him again. Each woman was allowed space at the shelter for a month while she got legal help and made new living arrangements. Hard cases were allowed to stay a little longer. She said she was sorry, but he was the sweetest man, and when he loved her up, it was the only time she knew heaven.

Carol felt humiliated. Once each week the women lined up and were given their food: three very small whole frozen chickens, a package of pork hot dogs, some plain-wrap cans of baked beans,

eggs, milk, margarine, white bread. The children were happy with
the food. Carol's sons played in the courtyard with the other children. Carol had difficulty relating to the other mothers. One had ten
children. Two had black eyes. Several were pregnant. She began to
have doubts that what Bard had done had been violent enough to
cause her to run away. Did mental violence or violence done to furniture really count as battering? She wondered if she had been too hard
on her husband. She wondered if she hadn't been wrong to come
here. All he had done—he said so himself, on the taped conversations, dozens of times—was to break a lousy hundred-dollar table.
He had broken it before; he had fixed it before. Why was this time
different from any of the others? She had pushed all his buttons,
that's all, and he had gotten mad, and he had pulled the table away
from the wall and smashed off its legs and thrown the whole thing
outside into the yard. Then he had put his head through the wall,
using the top of his head as a battering ram. He had knocked open a
hole to the other side. Then he had bitten his youngest son on the
scalp. What was so terrible about that? It was just a momentary
thing. He didn't mean anything by it. When his son had begun to cry
in fear and pain, hadn't he picked the child up and told him it was
nothing? If she would just come home he would never get angry
again. They'd have their sweet life. They'd go to a picnic, a movie,
the beach. They'd have it better than ever before. He had just started
going to a new church that was helping him to become a kinder and
more sensitive man. He was a better person than he had ever been; he
now knew the true meaning of love. Wouldn't she come back?

One day Bard called me and said, "Hey, the cops are here. You
didn't send them, did you?"

"Me?" I said. I turned on the tape recorder. "What did you do?"

"Nothing. I busted up some public property. Can you come down
and bail me out?"

"How can I?" I said. "My children. . . ."

"How can you *not?*"

I hung up and called Carol at the shelter. I told her, "I think he's
being arrested."

"Pick me up," she said, "and take me to the house. I have to get some things. I'm sure they'll let me out of the shelter if they know he's in jail. I'll check to make sure he's really there. I have to get us some clean clothes, and some toys for the boys. I want to get my picture albums. He threatened to burn them."

"You want to go to the house?"

"Why not? At least we know he's not going to be there. At least we know we won't find him hanging from a beam in the living room."

We stopped at a drugstore a few blocks away and called the house. No one was there. We called the jail. They said their records showed that he had been booked but they didn't know for sure whether he'd been bailed out. "Is there any way he can bail out this fast?" Carol asked.

"Only if he uses his own credit card," the man answered.

"I *have* his credit card," Carol said to me after she hung up. "We're so much in debt that I had to take it away from him. Let's just hurry. I hate this! I hate sneaking into my own house this way."

I drove to the house and we held hands going up the walk. "I feel his presence is here, that he's right here seeing me do this," she said, in the dusty, eerie silence of the living room. "Why do I give him so much power? It's as if he knows whatever I'm thinking, whatever I'm doing. When he was trying to find the children, I thought he had eyes like God, and he would go directly to the school where they were and kidnap them. I had to warn them, 'If you see your father anywhere, run and hide. Don't let him get near you!' Can you imagine telling your children that about their father? Oh, God, let's hurry."

She ran from room to room, pulling open drawers, stuffing clothes into paper bags. I stood in the doorway of their bedroom, my heart pounding as I looked at their bed with its tossed covers, at the phone he used to call me. Books were everywhere on the bed — books about how to love better, how to live better, books on the occult, on meditation, books on self-hypnosis for peace of mind. Carol picked up an open book and looked at some words underlined in red. "*You can always create your own experience of life in a beautiful and enjoyable way if you keep your love turned on within you — regardless of what other people say or do,*" she read aloud. She tossed it down in disgust. "He's paying good money for these," she said. She kept blowing her nose.

"Are you crying?"

"No!" she said. "I'm allergic to all this dust."

I walked to the front door, checked the street for his car, and went into the kitchen.

"Look at this," I called to her. On the counter was a row of packages, gift-wrapped. A card was slipped under one of them. Carol opened it and read it aloud: "I have been a brute and I don't deserve you. But I can't live without you and the boys. Don't take that away from me. Try to forgive me." She picked up one of the boxes and then set it down. "I don't believe this," she said. "God, where are the children's picture albums! I can't *find* them." She went running down the hall. In the bathroom, I saw the boys' fish bowl, with their two goldfish swimming in it. The water was clear. Beside the bowl was a piece of notebook paper. Written on it in his hand were the words, *Don't give up, hang on, you have the spirit within you to prevail.*

Two days later he came to my house, bailed out of jail with money his mother had wired. He banged on my front door. He had discovered that Carol had been to the house. "Did *you* take her there?" he demanded. "*You* wouldn't do that to me, would you?" He stood on the doorstep, gaunt, hands shaking.

"Was she at the house?" I asked. "I haven't been in touch with her lately."

"Please," he said, his words slurred, his hands out for help. "Look at this." He showed me his arms; the veins in his forearms were black-and-blue. "When I saw that Carol had been home, I took the money my mother sent me for food and bought three packets of heroin. I wanted to OD. But it was lousy stuff, it didn't kill me. It's not so easy to die, even if you want to. I'm a tough bird. But please, can't you treat me like regular old me; can't you ask me to come in and have dinner with you? I'm not a monster. Can't anyone, *anyone,* be nice to me?"

My children were hiding at the far end of the hall, listening. "Wait here," I said. I went and got him a whole ham I had. I handed it to him where he stood on the doorstep and stepped back with distaste. Ask him in? Let my children see *this?* Who knew what a crazy man would do? He must have suspected that I knew Carol's exact where-abouts. Whenever I went to visit her at the shelter I took a circuitous route, always watching in my rearview mirror for his blue car. Now I had my tear gas in my pocket; I carried it with me all the time, kept it beside my bed when I slept. I thought of the things in my kitchen: knives, electric cords, mixers, graters, elements which could become white-hot and sear off a person's flesh.

He stood there like a supplicant, palms up, eyebrows raised in hope, waiting for a sign of humanity from me. I gave him what I could—a ham and a weak, pathetic little smile. I said, dishonestly, "Go home, maybe I can reach her today, maybe she will call you once you get home." He ran to his car, jumped in it, sped off, and I thought, coldly, *Good, I'm rid of him. For now we're safe.* I locked the door with three locks.

Later, Carol found among his many notes to her one which said, "At least your sister smiled at me, the only human thing that hap-pened in this terrible time. I always knew she loved me and was my friend."

He became more persistent. He staked out my house, not believing I wasn't hiding her. "How could I possibly hide her?" I said to him on the phone. "You know I wouldn't lie to you."

"I know you wouldn't," he said. "I trust you." But on certain days I saw his blue car parked behind a hedge a block away, saw him hunched down like a private eye, watching my front door. One day my husband drove away with one of our daughters beside him, and an instant later the blue car tore by. I got a look at him then, curved over the wheel, a madman, everything at stake, nothing to lose, and I felt he would kill, kidnap, hold my husband and child as hostages till he got my sister back. I cried out. As long as he lived he would search for her, and if she hid, he would plague me. He had once said to her (she told me this), "You love your family? You want them alive? Then you'd better do as I say."

On the day he broke the table, after his son's face crumpled in ter-ror, Carol told him to leave. He ran from the house. Ten minutes later he called my sister and said, in the voice of a wild creature, "I'm watching some men building a house, Carol. I'm never going to build a house for you now. Do you know that?" He was panting like an animal. "And I'm coming back for you. You're going to be with me one way or the other. You know I can't go on without you."

She hung up and called me. "I think he's coming back to hurt us."

"Then get out of there," I cried, miles away and helpless. "Run!"

By the time she called me again I had the number of the shelter for her. She was at a gas station with her children. Outside were two phone booths—she hid her children in one; she called the shelter from the other. I called the boys at the number in their booth and I read to them from a book called *Silly Riddles* while she made arrangements to be taken in. She talked for almost an hour to a counselor at the shelter. All the time I was sweating and reading riddles. When it was settled, she came into the children's phone booth and we made a date to meet in forty-five minutes at Sears so she could buy herself some underwear and her children some blue jeans. They were still in their pajamas.

Under the bright flourescent lights in the department store, we looked at price tags, considered quality and style, while her teeth chattered. Our eyes met over the racks, and she asked me, "What do you think he's planning now?"

My husband got a restraining order to keep him from our doorstep, to keep him from dialing our number. Yet he dialed it, and I answered the phone, almost passionately, each time I heard it ringing, having run to the room where I had the tape recorder hooked up. "Why is she so afraid of me? Let her come to see me without bodyguards! What can happen? The worst I could do is kill her, and how bad could that be, compared with what we're going through now?"

I played her that tape. "You must never go back," I said. She agreed; she had to. I brought clean nightgowns to her at the shelter; I brought her fresh vegetables, and bread that had substance.

Bard had hired a psychic that last week, and had gone to Las Vegas to confer with him, bringing along a $500 money order. When he got home, he sent a parcel to Las Vegas, containing clothing of Carol's and a small gold ring which she often wore. A circular that Carol found later under the bed promised immediate results: *Gold has the strongest psychic power—you can work a love spell by burning a red candle and reciting, "In this ring I place my spell of love to make you return to me." This will also prevent your loved one from being unfaithful.*

Carol moved across the street from my house just before Halloween. We devised a signal so she could call me for help in case some maniac cut her phone lines. She would use the antique gas alarm which our father had given to me. It was a loud wooden clacker which had been used in the war. She would open her window and spin it. I could hear it easily. I promised her that I would look out of my window often and watch for suspicious shadows near the bushes under her windows. Somehow, neither of us believed he was really gone. Even though she had picked up his wallet at the morgue, the wallet he'd had with him while he breathed his car's exhaust through a vacuum cleaner hose, thought his thoughts, told himself she didn't love him and so he had to do this and do it now, even though his ashes were in the dumpster, we felt that he was still out there, still looking for her.

Her sons built a six-foot-high spider web out of heavy white yarn for a decoration, and nailed it to the tree in her front yard. They built a graveyard around the tree, with wooden crosses. At their front door they rigged a noose, and hung a dummy from it. The dummy, in their father's old blue sweatshirt with a hood, swung from the rope. It was still there long after Halloween, still swaying in the wind.

Carol said to me, "I don't like it, but I don't want to say anything to them. I don't think they're thinking about him. I think they just made it for Halloween, and they still like to look at it."

Witnesses

My mother called early on Thanksgiving morning to tell me she didn't want any transients at her funeral. I was surprised to hear her voice since she was coming over later for dinner with all the relatives and we usually didn't have our daily long talk by phone when she was actually scheduled to arrive here. We both understood that *some* news needed to be saved for when we were face-to-face.

"Your Aunt Gert—," she said, with contempt in her voice, "she's been reading obituaries in the newspaper and she wants all that flowery baloney when she dies: 'Adored wife, beloved sister, devoted daughter, cherished aunt.' But I want absolutely none of that. Just my name, if anything. With the words, 'Private services.' I don't want a bunch of strangers gawking at me, crying crocodile tears. I haven't got a friend in the world! All those people who knew me from the antique store when Daddy was alive—they're all nothing to me. They never call me. They never want to know how I am. So I don't want them at my funeral, coming back to your house for a party in my honor, Janet, stuffing themselves with food that you pay a fortune for, and pretending they're heartbroken that I'm dead."

I stopped myself from pointing out to my mother that she didn't even like me to have parties in her honor when she was *alive*. She was always against my having Thanksgiving dinner; we had the same argument every year. "Why knock yourself out? Your Aunt Gert and I could just as happily stay home. She'll cook some garlicky thing for Uncle Harry at their place, and I'll stay here and put a chicken pie in the oven, and I'll read the paper, and I'll have a nice quiet day to myself."

The vision appalled me: my mother, alone in her little apartment on Thanksgiving Day, just like all the other days she was alone there; the world revving up for the holidays, cars filling freeways, families traveling to visit together, and my mother alone with the LA *Times,* and her pale little chicken pie burning around the edges in her uneven oven.

"I've already bought an eighteen-pound turkey," I told my mother on the phone, "and it was really cheap; there's a price war going on. So don't worry about that."

"Don't you hate to handle a dead turkey?" my mother asked. "They're so cold and slippery." She paused. "Did I ever tell you," she said, in a totally different tone of voice, "that the first week Daddy and I were married I tried to cook a chicken? And I left all the giblets in the brown butcher paper in the neck of the bird? Daddy said to me, when I served him, 'What's this? Baked paper? A new kind of stuffing?' " My mother giggled. She sounded no more than seventeen.

"You have to come," I said. "We have to have your birthday party." My mother's birthday fell just after Thanksgiving every year. I always baked her a chocolate cake, and wrote her age on it in whipped cream.

The sound of her voice changed again. "Why should you go to all that trouble?" she asked, almost angrily. "What for? So we can get crumbs all over your rug, and give you and Danny a big headache? I don't want you cleaning up for us. You have other important things to do."

"What could be more important than having everyone together? And this year Carol lives right across the street." There was another pause as my mother struggled with her thoughts. I wondered if she was going to say it. She did.

"At least *he* won't be there with all his craziness."

Taking my silence for criticism, she said defensively: "You remember how he always walked right in and started looking for wine in the refrigerator! Don't you remember? It always annoyed you.

The way he would start eating before we all sat down. The way his eyes darted around?"

What I was remembering was something a little different about what happened last Thanksgiving when Bard, my sister's husband, was still alive, when my sister's eyes hadn't taken on that hollow look yet, though even at that time she was full of fear. It had started to rain very hard during dinner, and Bard — in his nervous way — had leaped up to check on our new awning. Danny had just installed it the past summer, and in the sudden downpour the rain was puddling the rubbery plastic, weighting it down so it looked like a swollen belly about to burst.

"Get me a broom," Bard had instructed me from where he stood in the teeming rain on the blackening cement of the patio. "Get it now." An icy wind blew in the door. I exchanged a look with Carol. She said quietly, "Get it for him. He needs to be a hero."

Danny said sternly, "Don't worry about it," meaning that this was his house, his awning, his responsibility. But I got Bard the broom anyway, because I was afraid of what might result if we contradicted him. I could remember him standing out there in the darkness, his body outlined against explosive flashes of lightning, jousting at the heavy water balloon of the awning, poking it fiercely with the broomstick, deaf to the thunder and our calls to come in, till, finally, he pierced the awning and was nearly drowned in a cascade of freezing water. His hoarse scream, of shock, of disbelief, of failure, still echoed in my mind. I had had to give him Danny's bathrobe to wear during dinner; he sat there, limp, in my husband's yellow terry robe, his hair and beard wet, staring morosely down the length of the table. He sat alone at the far end, opposite me. The way the light fell on him, the way he looked so drawn, the way his beard lay sorrowfully on his face, made me think of Jesus. The next day, when the stores opened for Christmas sales, I bought Danny a new bathrobe and threw out the one Bard had worn at Thanksgiving dinner. Bard didn't kill himself till five months after that.

"It was pure luck that Carol found a house right across the street from you," my mother said now, on the phone. "Sisters should be near each other if they get along. Thank God you and Carol are not like Gert and me. Can you *believe* we're sisters? We have less in common than the Arabs and the Israelis. Carol is so thankful to have you to depend on right across the street. Now at least I can die in peace, knowing he's gone and won't be a danger to her. I know you'll take care of her and the boys. I know you'll do your best."

"I'll try," I said uncomfortably. "So let's all have a nice Thanksgiving dinner, Mom. Just come with Aunt Gert and Uncle Harry and put away your grievances and let's all try to have a happy time."

"Oh, God," Carol giggled, looking out my kitchen window. "Welcome to the Salvation Army." I wiped my hands and came to look out the window, where Uncle Harry and Aunt Gert were helping my mother out of the car. The three of them began to load up with paper bags and cartons and armloads of junk from the trunk to bring into the house.

"Boys," Carol called to her sons. "why don't you go out and help everyone carry in the stuff?" The boys, Abram, eleven (named for my father), and David, nine, were building a fire in the fireplace.

"Go," Carol instructed them. "There might be goodies for you, you never know."

"Yeah," David said, making a face. "Like the last time. They brought *cantaloupes*. They tasted terrible."

"They saw a big sale," Carol explained. "They can't resist bargains."

Aunt Gert was carrying a big silver tray in her arms as she came up the walk. She had insisted on bringing the stuffing. She called three times last night while she was making it. "Do I have to use mushrooms?" she had asked on the first call. "Your recipe calls for mushrooms." "It would be nice," I said. On the second call she asked, "I only have canned mushrooms, fresh are too expensive; will that be all right?" "Fine," I said. The third call informed me that she had chosen to do without the mushrooms. "The Pilgrims probably didn't use them," she said. "How could they know which ones were poisonous and which ones weren't? So I'm sure they didn't use them at all."

Danny, who loved my stuffing and looked forward all year to Thanksgiving, wanted me to make my own recipe and pull a quick switch just before dinner, but I told him he would just have to bear up and make some sacrifices like the rest of us. "I'll make my own recipe tomorrow, when they've all gone home. We'll have our own private Thanksgiving with the leftovers," I had promised him.

As my relatives, laden like nomads, squeezed through the front door, I wondered if I was wishing this day were over and they had all gone home already. I was feeling the strain of having been up since six o'clock to put in the turkey. I'd been cleaning and cooking for hours without a rest. I was sorry I had bothered to dust, since now my mother, aunt, and uncle were covering every available surface with their bags and boxes and armloads of offerings.

"Bear up," Carol whispered to me, squeezing my arm. I looked over at Danny, afraid that he might do what he once threatened to do, go outside and bring in a huge trash can and suggest that they all immediately toss everything they had brought directly into it.

"Don't kiss me," my mother said. "I think I may be getting a sore throat." She was wearing big plastic sunglasses, which hid half her face. The part of it I could see was small and delicate. Her chin was pointed, her cheekbones sunken. Her white short hair looked pixie-ish and gleamed like fresh snow.

"Your hair looks nice, Mom," I said.

"Your aunt says I look like a pinhead," she snorted in Gert's direction. "She'd like me to have one of those bouffant beehives she's so fond of."

"No, I wouldn't," Aunt Gert said. "It's just too severe that way. It's not feminine."

"You and your ruffles," my mother said.

Aunt Gert was wearing a black wool cape with white piping, which matched her white hair. She was busy unloading things from a paper bag and handing articles to Carol's sons. "This I got at a City of Hope luncheon, little table favors. I thought you boys could play with them." Carol's sons exchanged glances. Aunt Gert handed them each a little pink plastic cow with a bell around its neck. "And where is Danny?" she asked, with an artificial lilt in her voice. My husband stepped forward. "This is for you." She handed him an article torn from the *Reader's Digest* about saving money on taxes. Danny thanked her.

Now it was my mother's turn. She had fancier gifts: extra rolls of paper towels that had been on sale, a gallon jar of apple juice she'd never use because it was much too big for her, some bars of soap, some cans of tuna fish. She always cleaned out her cupboards for us. With a flourish she held up three boxes of macaroni-and-cheese dinners. "Who can use these? Carol? Janet?" Ready for this, we both answered together, with enthusiasm. "*I* can use them!"

"Well, you'll just have to share them," my mother said. I was feeling giddy. I grabbed the boxes and handed one to Carol, put one down on the rug for myself. The third one I opened up, ripping the cardboard top, and telling Carol to hold out her hand. Laughing, I poured half of the elbow macaroni into her cupped palm. Her sons giggled as the noodles spilled over onto the rug.

"Listen," I said to my mother, "fair is fair, Mom. I don't want you to play favorites. One-and-a-half boxes for me, one-and-a-half for Carol. Share and share alike."

Even my mother was smiling. "That's what I like to see," she said. "Sisters who get along. So when I die, there won't be any quarreling over who gets what."

Aunt Gert made an angry noise. "Your mother is so *negative*," she said fiercely. "She likes to spoil everyone's good time." She began to hold up more of *her* contributions. Coupons, for one thing. She loved to offer us coupons from the newspaper for fifteen cents off on margarine, fifty cents off on detergent. "With double coupons," she instructed, "you can really save a lot." Carol groaned. "I hate coupons," she said. "I stand there in the market and they go flying all over the floor, and they're always expired, or they're for the super-jumbo size, or the check-out lady tells me I didn't cut the edges straight enough."

"You have no right to be fussy," Aunt Gert said, her voice unforgiving. "You, in your situation, can't turn down the chance to save a few pennies." She looked over at my mother. "You haven't raised your children right," she said. "They're spoiled. They think the world owes them a living."

"I'm sure you could have done better with them," my mother shot back, her eyes flashing. "If you're so smart, you should have had children of your own."

"I wasn't as lucky as you," Gert said. Then she looked at Uncle Harry, who was standing slope-shouldered and a little dazed, still wearing his coat, in the living room. "But God was good to me, I was blessed with two good husbands, even if I married late in life."

"Hi," Myra said, coming down the hall. Everyone turned to look at her. I knew immediately what my aunt was thinking: that it was a shame such adolescent beauty was wasted on such a sloppy child. She was examining Myra's shapeless oversized sweater (it happened to have belonged to Bard; she had claimed his wool sweater, his black raincoat, his sleeping bag, on the day my sister was throwing everything in cartons for the Salvation Army). Aunt Gert was frowning at Myra's non-hairdo—lank blonde hair hanging in her face. She was thinking how much prettier that face would be with a little make-up on it. I prayed she wasn't going to ask Myra again if she was using acne medication; that would be the end of Myra for the day. I would have to bring her a turkey leg in her room.

"How about a little vitamin for your old aunt?" she asked. Myra dipped her head grudgingly and stepped forward to peck Aunt Gert on the cheek. "Did I ever tell you . . . ," Aunt Gert asked Myra for at least the millionth time, ". . . that when your mommy was a little girl she used to come over to me and say, 'Could I give you a vitamin?' and then she'd kiss me on the elbow? She used to call it *belbow!*"

"I know," Myra said. She looked around at the junk on the coffee tables. She turned and went down the hall toward her room.

"Remember to turn off the lights when you're not in a room!" Aunt Gert called after her. "Later I'm going to spank your little bottom if I find lights on all over the house and no one in the rooms." Myra grunted. She held the opinion that Aunt Gert used the checking-on-lights excuse to check the condition of the bedrooms. She was probably right. As a precaution, I always made my bed before Aunt Gert visited. Myra refused to be manipulated—she considered her room her sacred, private space. She was willing for Aunt Gert to think ill of her; she was braver than me.

"A cold soul," Aunt Gert said to me in Yiddish. "Why doesn't she have your affectionate disposition?" She looked at Danny, as if the fault was evident in his half of the genes.

"Fifteen is a hard age, Aunt Gert. I think you remember me being affectionate when I was very small. I don't think I sat in anyone's lap when I was fifteen."

"At fifteen you had already met Danny. I'll bet you were in his lap, plenty."

Danny about-faced and walked down the hall. I heard our bedroom door close quietly. Uncle Harry said, wisely, "Myra misses her sisters."

"This has been a hard year for her," I said. I was referring to all her losses; one sister marrying, one sister gone to college, Danny's father dying of cancer, Bard's suicide. Two schoolmates of hers had also died in terrible accidents. Suddenly I felt it had been a hard year for me, too. I went over to my mother and put an arm around her frail shoulders. She was rummaging around in a plastic bag for newspaper articles she had clipped which she thought would be of interest to me. She lost her balance and fell against me. I led her to the couch and sat her down. I had a memory of walking with my grandmother that way, when she was very old, and I was about ten.

Something flashed in Aunt Gert's mind as well, for she said, "You ought to wear flat shoes, Anna; remember how vain Mama was? She didn't like those black old-lady oxfords with laces. She refused to wear them. Remember when she turned her heel and fell? That time we couldn't pick her up, even the two of us? We had to run across the street and get the painter down from his ladder to help pick Mama up."

"I remember," my mother said warily, waiting for what was coming next.

"So you shouldn't wear those shoes." My mother was wearing high heels because of an arthritic spur on her instep; flat heels caused her pain. She reminded Aunt Gert of this. "I can't even go to the bathroom in the morning without putting on heels."

"But you're looking for trouble in more ways than one," Aunt Gert reminded her. "Remember what that man said?"

"What man?" I asked, and Aunt Gert was satisfied. Now my mother would have to tell the truth about her heels. My mother smiled in spite of herself.

"I was walking in the parking lot of City College, where I take my music class, and a young man came up behind me and said, 'You really shouldn't walk like that around here.' "

"She swings her fanny," Aunt Gert explained. "And in that neighborhood — there was a rape of an 80-year-old woman in one of the bathrooms on campus last year — your mother shouldn't let her skirt swish around."

"Can I help it if my skirt swishes?" my mother said, and we all laughed. Carol laughed with us and then continued to laugh hysterically. She couldn't seem to stop. My mother was pleased. Aunt Gert was chastened. I noticed she was wearing modified old-lady oxfords, with little silver Pilgrim buckles on them.

"I'm hungry," Abram said. "When do we eat?" He and his brother, David, had made a four-foot pile of logs in the fireplace. There wasn't even room to get a match between the layers of wood.

"Oh — ," Aunt Gert said, "I'd better get this stuffing into the oven to warm. By the way, Janet, did you tell me to *boil* the onions and celery or brown them first?"

"Brown them."

"Well, I boiled them. But what's the difference?"

The table looked elegant. I had unpacked the crystal water tumblers from the antique store, the Limoges turkey platter my father had given me, the hand-painted celery-and-olive dish, the hand-carved napkin rings of burnished wood with tendrils of lily-of-the-valley curling around them. The brass candlesticks were gleaming; the points of flame on the red candles were shooting out stars of light. I had outdone myself, it was true. I was using all the precious things I had kept hidden for the last few years. I wondered if Carol would notice. In the past, when Bard had come to our Thanksgiving dinners, something always got broken, either by accident or by design. He had a tendency to test things, to challenge their strength. Or to balance delicate dishes, one upon the other. Or to clink a glass too powerfully in making a toast to a happier, more prosperous year for all of us. I counted only him missing; my father had been dead so long that I no longer saw him looming, bigger than life, like a Thanksgiving Day Parade balloon, over the table. And yet the thought of him triggered the memory of what I had dreamed last night. I closed my eyes to shut out the shimmer of the flickering candles. In my dream my father had told me that he had discovered the cause of his leukemia: little colorful plastic elephants and dinosaurs, like the kind found in babies' teething rings, were bobbing along in his bloodstream; his blood was transparent as water. But he was also cured! He had discovered that the cure for cancer was embalming fluid! My father sat up in his coffin to tell me this amazing discovery; his hands held to the sides of the casket as they might have held to the edges of a rowboat.

"The trouble," he said in the dream, "is that they cut out my heart during the autopsy. Even though I'm cured now, I can't live. Your mother gave away my heart too easily." I looked down the length of the table to where my mother was holding her wine glass in her quivery fingers, and remembered her fear and guilt on the day she had signed the autopsy papers for the entreating physician.

"Let's have a toast," Danny said, raising his wine glass. Myra raised her glass higher than anyone.

"To life," Aunt Gert said.

"To health," my mother said.

"To love," Myra said.

"To less inflation," Uncle Harry said.

"To all of us," Danny said. "To Bonnie and her husband, and to Jill away at college, too."

"And let us all be here again next year," my sister said.

"And to those we love who aren't here anymore," I added, feeling my eyes fill unexpectedly.

"Pass the turkey," David said. He reached across the table and knocked over the gravy bowl. He apologized profusely. Myra, who was sitting next to him, hugged him hard with both arms, and kissed the top of his head.

"It's too bad we have no men in our family," Aunt Gert said as we cleared the table. What had brought this on was the fact that I had warned her not to drop anything down the sink, since the disposal had been broken for a month.

Abram, who was carrying in the platter with the remains of the turkey said, "My dad could have fixed it. He could fix anything."

"Danny plans to fix it," I said. "He just hasn't gotten around to it yet."

"We need more men," Aunt Gert continued, scraping turkey bones and yam skins into a garbage bag. "Our family is a world of women. My father died at forty-eight, so you never had a grandfather. Your own wonderful father is gone. My brother drowned at sea. You have no sons. You have no brothers. It's a wonder we can get along, all of us women without men."

"Maybe I can fix the disposal," Abram said. He was wearing a shirt with rocket ships on it. "I fixed our video game when it broke. Mom couldn't figure it out, but I fixed it."

"Carol buys them all the modern toys when she should be saving every penny," Aunt Gert whispered to me. "What is she going to do when all the money runs out?"

Since Abram had gone back to get more dishes, I told Aunt Gert that Carol felt her boys had been through a lot, that they deserved a few toys.

"She never should have married him in the first place," she whispered. "A hippie. His brain was all scrambled by drugs." She made a face.

"Who wants to play Scrabble?" my mother called from the other room.

"I'll beat the pants off you," Aunt Gert called back. To me she said, "Why isn't your mother bringing dishes in here? She's spoiled, that's why. She acts helpless in the kitchen. Did I ever tell you about the Thanksgiving when we were little and an uncle of ours brought us a chocolate turkey and told us to share it, and she wanted it for herself and she threw a tantrum?"

"I know that story."

"Your mother claims I made it up. She's always telling me I make things up because she doesn't remember my stories. Why should she remember when she had a tantrum? It's not the kind of thing she likes to remember about herself. It doesn't flatter her."

"People remember different things," I said. "Everyone's reality is different."

"Tell *her* that!" Aunt Gert said. "From you she might believe it. Everything *I* say she considers the words of a dummy."

"Come in and play, Gert," my mother called. "The board is all set up."

"What about dessert?" David demanded. "When do we get the birthday cake?"

"Shh," Carol said, "don't give away the surprise."

"We do this every year," David said loudly. "How can Mom-mom be surprised?"

"When you're old, your memory goes bad," my mother explained to him, "so every year I don't remember the year before. Although this year, I ought to stop counting. I'm too near the end to celebrate, don't you think?"

"We always have to celebrate life. And this is an important year, Anna, seventy-five," Aunt Gert said, taking my hand and pulling me with her into the dining room where the Scrabble board was now sitting on the table among the crumbs and cranberry stains on my linen tablecloth.

"Seventy-five?" my mother said, puzzled. But then she got busy picking her Scrabble tiles, and within the first ten minutes of the game she made an eight-letter, triple-score word: *quixotic*.

"Tell me something about my great-grandmother," Myra asked Aunt Gert while my mother was taking her time finding her next super-score word. Aunt Gert leaned forward and held Myra's hair off her face. "Just one barrette, darling, it would show off your pretty face. Why do you want to look like a sheepdog?"

Myra brushed her hand away. "Was she smart?"

Aunt Gert looked over at my mother. "Was Mama smart? No, I don't think so. She was a peasant woman. Very practical, down to earth. When she couldn't sleep, she'd get up and wash the floor or bake a cake. She never sat around dreaming. She wasn't affectionate, either."

"She was never affectionate," my mother agreed. She made the word *syzygy* on the board, using a blank for one of the *y*'s.

"She never taught us anything philosophical," Aunt Gert said, arranging and rearranging her tiles. "She just made sure we were well dressed, and neat, and always clean. She never let us out of the house unless every button was closed. That's why I take great pride in my appearance to this day. Even if I get my clothes at bargain prices, no one knows. I always look good."

"Mama was very vain," my mother said.

"That's who you get it from," Aunt Gert suggested. She made the word *banjo*. "Remember, in the rest home, she wouldn't let anyone come to visit her unless she had her earrings in. There was one pair she loved best of all — your Abram had given them to her from his antique store — a little cluster of gold flowers with a diamond in the center."

"I remember them," my mother said.

"She used to have the nurse put them in her ears every day. They weren't really nurses, they were the worst-paid help for those hard jobs they had to do. When I first saw that home, it smelled so of *pishachs* I ran out screaming. I kept Mama home for eight months after that, caring for her myself, until I collapsed. I couldn't even turn her over anymore, or change her sheets."

"Didn't she lose those earrings?" my mother asked.

"Lose them! Don't you remember what happened? One of her hands was paralyzed, all the fingers were curled up. And one day, with her good hand, she dropped the earrings into the cup of her paralyzed hand, intending to have the attendant put them in her ears. But it was a new girl. She took Mama to the bathroom and was about to put Mama on the toilet from the wheelchair, when she saw the earrings in her hand; and thinking they were a clump of toilet paper or something useless, she just grabbed them away from Mama's hand and tossed them in the toilet and flushed them away."

"Oh, now I remember," my mother said.

"How could you forget! Mama couldn't be consoled for days."

"Abram got her a new pair."

"They didn't have real diamonds. You wouldn't let him give her real diamonds. You said the help at the home would steal them."

"I don't remember that."

"It's the kind of thing you don't remember," Aunt Gert said. "Believe me, though. I never forget anything important."

"You and an elephant," my mother said.

"Danny and Uncle Harry were sitting at opposite ends of the

couch. Danny suggested, "Would you like to play a game of chess?"
Uncle Harry answered, "Why not? It wouldn't be the worst idea."

In the kitchen I looked with despair upon the turkey carcass, the
leftover stuffing (nearly all of it), the plates of cranberry sauce, the
half-full salad bowl, the greasy roasting pan. I had ten hours of work
ahead of me there. Where was Carol? I checked the bathrooms, the
bedrooms. I heard her boys shouting in the yard where they were
throwing a Frisbee. I took my jacket off its hook by the door and
went outside to find Carol standing at the far end of the yard, under
the sharp and leafless branches of the plum tree. I came up beside her
and put my arm around her.

"I'm okay," she said, but when she turned to look at me I saw tears
in her eyes. "I'm really okay. I've been doing really well. I was just
remembering how he once said he was going to paint a clown's face
on himself and then shoot himself through its red mouth. He was going to die laughing at the world. He said he didn't want me to identify
his body, though. It would be too much of a mess. He didn't want me
to be disturbed." She laughed, and tears rolled down her face. I
wiped them away with my fingers. "But I haven't been thinking of
him, really. I just did, suddenly, that's all."

"You can think of him. It's all right."

"I dreamed he was on the other side of a glass wall last night, with
Skippy. He was threatening to slit the dog's throat. He had a knife.
He did. He killed my dog. But I couldn't go out there to save him."

I stood with Carol in the chill air, and we watched her boys running through the grass. "I'm so afraid for them," she said. "How will
I ever know how much this whole thing has damaged them?"

"You just have to love them and do what you can," I said. "And I'll
be here to help."

"You better live a long time," she said. "I'm counting on you."

"I'll do my best."

"Hey, Mommy, catch." David whirled the white Frisbee at us, and
Carol lunged for it. She smiled when he called to her, "Great catch;
you're terrific."

"Do you think we ought to go in for the big birthday party?"

"Why not?" Carol said. "Since we can't stop Mom from getting older, we might as well celebrate the fact that she's still alive."

My mother's skirt was too tight; she and Aunt Gert were conspiring about what to do. "Come in the bedroom," Aunt Gert said, "and I'll cut the elastic."

"Don't go in *my* bedroom," Myra warned them. She added, "Don't worry, the light is out in there, I swear."

While my aunt and mother were in another part of the house, I got the cake ready. I mixed the heavy cream in a chilled silver bowl and added sugar and vanilla. The chocolate cake was three layers high, loaded with chocolate chips; it was beautiful. I embroidered my mother's age on the icing with whipped cream, licking my fingers. Seventy-five. What did it feel like to have lived that long? My mother had told me she read once that anyone who survived to the year 2000 could easily live to be one hundred. I didn't want to think about myself as old as I would be in the year 2000. I called out, "Come on in, Mom," and I told Myra to coax Danny and Uncle Harry from their chess game to the table.

My mother and Aunt Gert came down the hall, arms linked, laughing. My mother was wearing the black raincoat which had belonged to Carol's husband.

"Hey!" Myra said. "You *did* go in my room."

"We didn't look around," Aunt Gert said, "although if I were your mother I wouldn't buy you another pair of socks until you hang up everything that's on the floor of your room. She's too good to you."

"I had to take off my tight skirt," my mother said, flipping open the raincoat and letting us look briefly at her shapely legs. "Gert has to cut the elastic and add a piece before we go home. So I have nothing on." She giggled.

Aunt Gert added, "My sister, the flasher!" They smiled at each other. "It's a good thing for her I can sew."

"Sit down and don't disappear. I'll be right back," I said.

In the kitchen I lit the candles. There were two number-candles, a *seven* and a *five,* and then one plain birthday candle, the one to grow on. Lifting the cake platter, I marched into the living room, singing

"Happy Birthday" to my mother. Everyone joined in as my mother leaned forward to make her wish. She took a long time to think of one. Then she blew; she blew again and again, long and hard, her mouth a dark tunnel. The angle was wrong. The points of fire quivered but grew tall again. The boys begged their mother with a glance to be allowed to help; then they assisted, pushy in their certainty, blowing so hard that they tipped the candles over, extinguishing them like trees downed in a hurricane.

"May you live to be a hundred," Aunt Gert said.

My mother snapped, "Don't wish it on me."

"When I die," Aunt Gert said, "I want an open casket. I want everyone to see me and cry over me."

"I want mine closed," my mother said. "I don't want anyone grabbing a loudspeaker and shouting to the world 'She's gone!' "

"I want everyone I know at my funeral."

"I want only my children there," my mother said. "I know I mean something to *them*."

"You don't want *me* to be there?" Aunt Gert asked.

"I imagined I would be at yours, looking in your open casket," my mother said.

They stared at each other.

"I'm two years younger than you," Aunt Gert said finally. "So, since we can't know what God has in mind, you better let me know now if I'm invited."

"You're invited," my mother said, "as long as you don't make any flowery speeches."

"Time for presents," David interrupted. "Then we can eat the cake." He came running to my mother and handed her a small white box.

"What could it be?" my mother said, "I wonder what on earth it could be." She took off her huge sunglasses and laid them on the table beside the cake. "Don't tell me, my very favorite thing, a chocolate turkey!" She leaned forward and kissed David. Abram stepped forward and held up an identical box. "This is an extra turkey for Aunt Gert so she doesn't feel bad."

"Oh you darling!" Aunt Gert said. "Come over here to me, you precious child, and I'll give you a big kiss. Did I ever tell you about your grandmother's tantrum? It always used to kill her to share anything!"

"Is that so?" my mother said, her eyes looking very small. She opened her box roughly and pulled out her chocolate turkey. She laid it on the white tablecloth and brought her fist down upon it so hard that it crumbled into tiny pieces. "Here, I'm sharing." She handed the first and biggest piece to her sister. "Maybe this will make up to you for what you suffered at my hands." She looked at Carol. "You take the second-biggest piece. You should have some sweetness in your life for a change." The next pieces went to my mother's grandsons, the fatherless boys. She gave away the thin broken shell of her turkey till there were only a few crumbs left for her. She gathered them up by brushing them off the edge of the table into the white box. She closed the lid, and set the box aside.

"I don't want any transients at my funeral," she announced to Gert. "Don't get on the phone and start calling everyone you ever met at bus stops or at card parties or in the Jewish bakery. I planned my own wedding and I have a right to want what I want at my own funeral."

"Okay, okay," Aunt Gert said. "Calm down. Don't get into a fit. You might have a stroke, like Mama."

"I just want everyone to hear. You are all witnesses. So don't dress me up in some lace gown and put me on display like a store dummy."

"Believe me, I couldn't care less what you do when you're dead," Aunt Gert said. She took a small bite of her fragment of chocolate. "Come back to the bedroom and I'll fix your skirt so you don't go home naked like Lady Godiva."

When they came down the hall a while later, we were all watching slides of the children when they were little. My aunt and mother were engaged in an argument about who was wearing the outfit that cost the least. They sat together on the couch, Gert and Anna, sisters, and debated over the whir of the slide projector.

"I got this blouse for fifty cents at a rummage sale," Aunt Gert said. "It's a thirty-dollar blouse."

"My skirt was seventy-five cents at the thrift shop," my mother said. "And my shoes, one dollar."

"My slip was a dime," Aunt Gert said. "My whole *outfit* was only two-fifty."

"Well," Carol interrupted. "You think that's cheap? *My* dress was one-fifty at Goodwill. It must be in my blood. I never wear anything that isn't a tremendous bargain."

Uncle Harry and Danny were making goggle eyes at one another, but smiling just the same. Then on the screen I saw my father, in the bloom of health, riding on a broomstick across a wide green meadow, with my firstborn, Bonnie, beside him on her hobby horse. She was three. He was fifty-five, in the last year of his life. Click. There I was, at only twenty-seven, my hair in a long braid, wearing pink stretch pants and pointy-toed sneakers. I felt Danny come up beside me and put his hand on my shoulder. He leaned down. "You were so cutie then," he whispered in my ear. "I remember exactly how you looked then, *exactly!*"

Click. My mother and father appeared in front of me, sitting on our swingset. My mother was on my father's lap—he was pumping the way he taught me to do, with legs out wide—and my mother's delicate legs were hanging down inside his. She looked frightened. Click. There was Bard, holding Myra upside down by her red sausage-legs-in-tights. He was grinning into the sun, his eyes red as a wolf's.

"I remember that day," Myra said. "I remember it perfectly clearly."

"Me too," David piped up from a corner of the darkened room.

"You can't remember it," Carol said softly. "You weren't born yet."

"Well, it feels like I remember it," he said. "So if I want to I will."

The slides went by faster as Uncle Harry clicked the remote control button. Time shot by in a blur; I had one child, two children, three. Danny was young and strong, Danny was a little heavier, Danny had gray hair. The Thanksgiving dinner scenes came into view, ten years in a row. The hair of Aunt Gert and my mother became whiter and whiter. The people changed; children were added, parents subtracted. Bard, the last year, was there at the head of the table with a halo of light around his head, staring at us with his red, tortured, recessed eyes. And there was my mother and her various birthday cakes—devil's food, chocolate chip, fudge, mocha cream—and her mouth open and blowing, as if she were trying to extinguish the world.

"Mommy," Myra stood in front of me, bending to whisper into my ear. "Mom-mom is seventy-six on this birthday, not seventy-five. I counted from the year she was born. We made a mistake."

I closed my eyes and counted. "You're right," I agreed, "but let's not say anything and get everyone upset."

"But you know what that means," Myra insisted. "It means that she didn't get her one candle to grow on."

I got up quietly, and taking my daughter's hand I led her into the kitchen. While the light from the slide projector flickered and flashed like lightning in the room beyond, I enacted a little ceremony with Myra, lighting one candle for my mother, the one to grow on, and letting Myra blow it out.

ILLINOIS SHORT FICTION